COULD IT BE MURDER?

Last year's May Day celebrations ended in tragedy for Gemma with the mysterious death of her Aunt Clara. Having inherited her aunt's run-down cottage in her childhood village of Wythorne, Gemma moves in, hoping to investigate the death, and is drawn to Brad, the local pub owner. But what she finds instead is a dead body, and a basket of poisonous mushrooms that have put her unsuspecting friend in hospital. Can Gemma get to the bottom of things before she and Brad become the next victims?

Books by Charlotte McFall
in the Linford Romance Library:

HEALING THE HURT
DIFFICULT DECISIONS
RETURN TO RIVER SPRINGS
WISH UPON A STAR

CHARLOTTE McFALL

COULD IT BE MURDER?

Complete and Unabridged

LINFORD
Leicester

First published in Great Britain in 2018

First Linford Edition
published 2019

A catalogue record for this book is available from the British Library.

ISBN 978–1–4448–4034–6

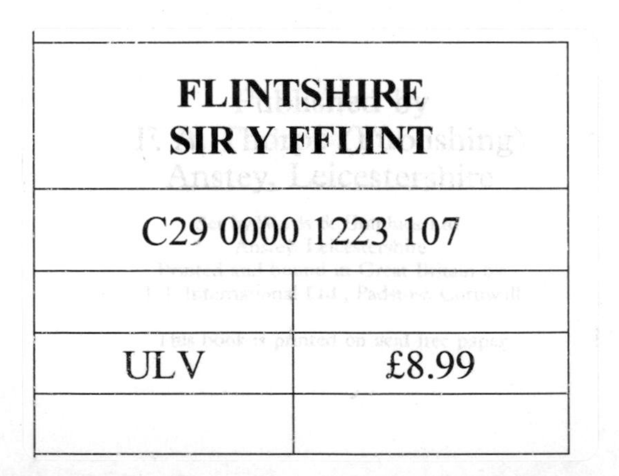

1

May 1, 2017

Clara Howarth walked out of St John's Church, making sure to lock the door securely and proudly holding on to her trophy. The wooden base was heavy for the small crystal vase, which sat neatly on the plinth.

The Charlotte Royale recipe she had taken from a TV show had won first place. One more win and she would beat Mrs Withenshaw's record of ten wins in the annual bake off. Wouldn't that be something for the village to talk about?

How she would like to wipe that smug look off old Mrs Withenshaw's face. It had taken over 30 years for Clara to win the same amount of trophies and now they lay neck and neck with 10 each.

Although Clara liked to come first, it was always nice when someone different won — it kept the villagers interested. After all, it was only a bit of fun as far as Clara was concerned.

Even her little Gemma had won once with a blackberry and apple pie, using handpicked blackberries and scrumped baking apples from Mr Timpson's farm. She smiled at the memory, but now Gemma had gone off to London and was working on a TV cookery show.

Clara was so proud of her great-niece, but she did miss her terribly. Gemma was never happy with village life. Perhaps one day they could once again share the old schoolhouse.

The sky had looked like blue had been painted on to blue as it grew darker. At least the rain had stopped, but this had made the old stone path rather slippery.

Just as Clara reached the stone entrance, she heard muffled voices and a shiver ran down her spine.

'There is no way her baking record will get beaten by that stuck-up Mrs Howarth. I will not allow it — do you understand?'

'Of course, but what can we do about it?' someone replied.

'Leave the details to me. You just do whatever I ask you to do.'

The voices faded into the distance. When Clara thought that whoever it was had gone, she hurried home as quickly as she could. It sounded as though she was in danger, but what could she do?

Would anyone believe the ramblings of a pensioner?

Clara sat in the comfy armchair by the fire. They had obviously been talking about Mrs Withenshaw, but surely they wouldn't sabotage Clara's next baking effort. Her gingerbread cake was to be next year's entry — another recipe from Gemma.

Clara was worried. Who were the two people she had heard?

Getting up to make a cup of tea, she

mulled over the snippets of overheard conversation and walked back into her living-room. She sat back down heavily in her chair, taking a sip of tea, her eyes closed.

Clara's body was found the next day. She was still sitting in her chair.

2

April, 2018

Gemma sat watching the minutes tick slowly by. The hands on the clock in the solicitor's office hadn't moved for what seemed like an eternity.

As far as she knew, her aunt who had recently passed away didn't have much. Until the solicitor's office rang her, Gemma han't even known Aunt Clara had made a will. It had never been discussed — not the topic of polite conversation.

It was already half past four in the afternoon and by six o'clock she needed to be halfway across London for the TV station's emergency meeting. Getting stuck in rush hour traffic and being late to the meeting wouldn't be the way to impress the bosses into keeping the cookery show on air.

Gemma approached the receptionist with caution. The woman behind the desk didn't look very friendly, and not the sort of person you wanted to interrupt when they were working.

'Excuse me, do you know if Mr Smithson will be much longer? I have a pressing engagement across town.'

'Not much longer,' the beady-eyed woman replied grumpily.

Gemma sat back down on one of the plush blue velvet chairs, taking a look at the large clock again.

Looking at the clock isn't going to make it go any faster, she thought to herself.

Just as Gemma was about to give up, the receptionist interrupted her quiet reflection.

'Mr Smithson will see you now.'

Well, half an hour late isn't too bad, Gemma thought.

She knocked on the door and on hearing 'Enter.' She walked in.

The room was manly in décor. Large

tomes adorned the bookcase which filled the entirety of one wall. A heavy oak desk sat in front of a large window. Two leather chairs sat either side of the desk, one occupied by a man — Mr Smithson, she presumed. A brown tatty armchair sat in one corner with a Tiffany-style lamp perched on a very precarious-looking table.

'Miss Howarth, I presume.' Mr Smithson stood, his hand outstretched.

Gemma walked towards him and accepted the greeting.

'Sit, please.'

Mr Smithson was a portly gentleman with a receding hairline. Gemma thought his face was kindly and honest-looking, although she had been wrong about people before.

He waited until she sat opposite him then sat down himself. Gemma smiled to herself.

Very gentlemanly, she thought. Not much of that around these days. It was hard enough to get a man to open a door for you, let alone wait until you had been seated before they sat themselves.

'Now, as you know, I called you here to read out your aunt's will. As you are her only living relative, everything she had will go to you.'

'Mr Smithson, I think you may have the wrong person. My aunt didn't actually own much of particular value — only sentimental things like her old piano.' Gemma was confused.

'On the contrary. Your aunt owned an old stone cottage in the village of . . . Wythorne, is it?' The solicitor paused to reread the name. 'That's in Lancashire, you know. That and all the house's contents are yours, and what little money she had goes to you.'

Gemma was astonished. She had always thought her aunt had rented the cottage.

'I . . . I didn't know.'

'No, I can see that. The cottage is in some state of disrepair. I can tell you, though, that an offer to purchase the cottage has been made. In fact, the party wants to purchase all the old cottages in that row.'

'Why would someone want to buy them all?' Gemma was curious. The cottages stood in the middle of the village and were once the old schoolrooms.

'That I cannot tell you, I'm afraid. I was approached last week to advise any relatives that the buyer would offer one hundred and fifty thousand pounds for the cottage.' He shuffled his paperwork and found the typewritten offer, handing the piece of paper to Gemma. 'I have considered it and for that cottage the offer is well below market value.'

Gemma held the offer, looking at it several times.

'Do you think I should accept?'

Mr Smithson stroked his chin.

'Well, that all depends on what you intend to do — go and live in it or leave it empty.'

'I'm going to have to give it some thought. I work in television and it would be used only at the weekends.'

'Here are the keys, and if you will sign the deeds I can file them and will leave it to you to decide what you would like to do.'

He stood up and shook hands with Gemma. She knew their meeting was over.

Maybe this weekend she would be able to go and see just how bad the cottage was and decide based on that.

She thanked him and left, rushing out of the building and out on to the busy street.

Trying to get a taxi in this traffic would be nigh on impossible, she thought, but then a taxi pulled up and its occupants got out. Gemma quickly rushed over.

'Can you take me to TV Centre as quickly as you can, please?'

A quick glance at her watch revealed she now had just half an hour to get across London. She felt sick. What did the station want? They had cancelled several programmes recently due to the recession. Would hers be another one to bite the dust to save that all-important cash?

There's no point second guessing, Gemma, she told herself, that isn't going to help.

A feeling of dread filled her as the taxi brought her closer and closer to the studio.

Yes, she was only a junior on the show, but a junior that did all the work. She devised the recipes, prepared all the ingredients and made the finished items.

That blonde-haired bimbo Queenie Mulligan received all the awards and praise for a wonderful show. Queenie would move on to presenting a new one and she would be all right. The ones left behind would be all the production assistants.

Gemma climbed out of the taxi and paid her fare. Rummaging around in her bag, she looked for her security pass.

One of these days, she thought to herself, she would clear this bag out.

Finally, in the darkest corner of her handbag, under tissues, pens, old make-up and a stack of receipts, Gemma found her security pass.

Checking her watch, she was surprised to find that it was only five-fifty, giving her ten minutes to get on to the right floor and past the security checks.

* * *

Gemma stood in the lift as it took her to the top floor. The walls were adorned with pictures of old television programmes that the studio had produced. One was a poster of her show: 'Queenie's Quick Meals'.

She loved working on the show. No two days were alike.

Her nerves jangled as she finally reached her floor. Stepping out of the lift, she was confronted by the chief executive of the studios.

'Ms Howarth, you have arrived at last.'

'Mr Gerard. How nice to see you

again.' Gemma held her hand out for him to shake but Mr Gerard just walked a little way in front of her, ignoring her proffered hand.

'Now, can we talk whilst we walk?'

Somehow Gemma didn't think it was a request but an order.

'Sure.' What she really wanted to say was, 'Just tell me what you want to say and let me go home. I'm tired, hungry and after the day I've had I would just rather hide under the duvet.'

Instead, she kept quiet and listened intently to what he said.

'Miss Howarth,' he began in his superior voice, 'as you know we have been restructuring the schedules, taking off those programmes whose ratings have fallen to an unacceptable level. I am sorry to tell you that your programme is one of those which we are taking off air.'

'You're what? Why? The show won best cookery show of the year last year. It's a highly rated show.' Gemma was agitated.

'It was, but 'Queenie's Quick Meals' is now a thing of the past. Obviously, all shows will be kept in the vault, but we won't be showing repeats for a long, long time.'

Gemma knew what that meant — no royalties for her, because she had been the real chef of the show. The presenter, Queenie Mulligan, couldn't boil an egg, let alone produce coq au vin.

Gemma handed him her security pass, and instead of continuing along the corridor with him, she turned to him and stood defiantly.

'I will go and clear my office.'

'Just make sure, Ms Howarth, that no office supplies end up in your boxes.'

With that, Mr Gerard turned on his shiny heel and walked into his office.

What on earth do they take me for, Gemma thought, incensed.

Storming into her office she began ripping things out of drawers, pulling things off the wall with such force that she even broke one of her picture frames.

'Well, it looks like I could be moving

into Aunt Clara's house after all,' she said aloud.

* * *

Gemma struggled down the stairs with her possessions. At least rush hour was nearly over so getting a taxi should be easy. She stood on the pavement for ten minutes before a taxi stopped for her. Half an hour later she was sitting in her flat.

Grabbing the books from the bookshelves, she shoved them almost carelessly into the boxes. What on earth had possessed her not to rent a flat of her own? The studio owned this one and without a show she could no longer stay here. She hadn't made many friends, and the ones she did have worked at the studio.

Gemma shook her head. No, they weren't really friends — just people that she worked with.

The security phone to her flat rang, making her jump. Who would be coming around now?

In her haste to answer, she dropped the phone on the floor. Grabbing the cable, she pulled it up.

'Louise. Yes, sure. Come on in.' The buzzer clicked, letting her know she had unlocked the main door.

Gemma was surprised that anyone would want to come and see if she was all right, and curious as to why Louise would bother.

Even though she was a friend, Louise was also the studio boss's cousin. Just a junior in the business really, graduating in the summer, she came and worked for the television studio.

It must be nice when you know people who can hand you a job just like that, Gemma thought with a grimace.

A quiet knock on the door alerted her to her guest. She slowly unbolted the door.

'Hey, Louise.'

'I can't believe what he has done.'

Gemma noted the sympathy in Louise's voice.

'Look, don't worry about it.'

'But what about the flat?'

'It belongs to the studio, and as I no longer work there, I can't live here.' Gemma put her finger to her mouth. 'But I found out today I have inherited a house and some money.' She sighed. 'I will be fine, so stop worrying about it.'

Louise shook her head.

'Gemma, you've worked so hard . . . '

'Drink?' Gemma asked, desperately trying to change the conversation because, no matter what Louise said, nothing could change what had happened.

'Sure. Coffee, please.'

'No worries.'

Gemma led them to the kitchen.

'How do you like your coffee?' she asked as she grabbed two cups out of the cupboard and turned the gas cooker on.

Gemma had always loved the sound of a whistling kettle, but they weren't to everyone's taste.

'Strong enough to stand a spoon in and black.' Louise perched herself on the edge of the kitchen table. 'Don't tell me you have forgotten already?'

'I'm sorry. My mind is everywhere at the minute.'

An ear-splitting whistle resonated around the room. Taking the kettle off the heat, Gemma poured the drinks as she listened to Louise's incessant chatter.

'You know, Gemma, your burrito recipe is so quick and easy. Gary and me, we have them every Saturday whilst he's watching football.'

Gemma smiled.

'That was the whole idea of 'Queenie's Easy Meals'. Even the people that can't cook can have a go at them.'

'True,' Louise conceded. 'But what am I going to do without your programme? I'm utterly useless in the kitchen.'

Gemma thought for a moment.

'Wait here a sec.' She dashed back

into the living-room, digging in one of the boxes, then pulled out a recipe book called 'Queenie's Quick Meals'.

Taking the book back into the kitchen, she gave it to Louise.

'Here, you can have this. I have other copies. Hopefully it will replace the TV show for you and at least you will be able to cook some things.'

It was beyond her how someone could survive without being able to cook, but in the era of ready meals and fast food restaurants it seemed it was all too common.

Louise smiled.

'Thanks, Gemma.'

Gemma was grateful that Louise had stopped by, and even more so when she drank her coffee and left, leaving her alone to pack her things. She didn't see the point in hanging around.

She probably could have stayed longer but decided against it. How long the studio would have let her keep the flat she didn't know. The last thing she needed was to come home one day to find the locks changed.

Gemma sighed heavily as she placed the last of her possessions into boxes. What she had would all fit in her car so there would be no need to hire a removal van. The flat came furnished so it was a case of black bags for her clothes and boxes for everything else.

Exhaustion finally consuming her, Gemma curled up on the sofa and fell asleep.

* * *

The sun had barely risen in the sky when she awoke. Slowly she packed her car up and left the flat keys with the building's caretaker.

It was best she set off now. It was only a three-hour drive; four if she took her time and stopped at the services on the way up.

Suddenly Gemma searched through her purse and realised she had no change for the toll booth at Watford Gap.

Oh, for goodness' sake. Can't anything go right for me, she asked herself.

3

Young, Free and Single

A Pint of your finest, Brad, please.'

'Coming right up, vicar.' Brad grabbed a beer glass and started pulling the beer. 'Have you heard about the cottages across the way?'

'Aye, some developer or other wants to buy the whole lot.' Rev Timpson picked up his pint. 'Disgraceful, if you ask me. Old Mrs Howarth's is empty so I bet that will be the first one to be sold off.'

'Did she have any relatives?' Brad looked at the vicar, wondering how he was always the first one to the bar after Sunday service. He never failed to surprise him. Nothing much changed in Wythorne.

'I believe she has a niece in television or some such,' the vicar replied, looking up briefly from his glass.

As more and more customers came through the door, Brad knew there would be no more time for chatter until the lunch rush was over. Many of them went into what used to be the old smoking room for peace and quiet from the children. He had kept the rule — no children allowed in the old snug. The smell of stale cigarette smoke still clung to the walls and deep into the old red plush chairs. He had given up trying to clean everything — it had become an expensive hobby, and nothing fixed the smell.

The pub looked just as it had when he was a young lad, not so long ago: the open fire against the main wall, copper bed-warming pans decorating the walls, with several old photographs of the surrounding countryside scattered in between.

The pub was stuck quite happily in a time warp, as was the rest of the village. But it was home. People were happy here and everyone knew everybody else, which was both a blessing and a curse. You couldn't do anything or go anywhere without people knowing what you were up to.

If you bought a new washing machine, everyone knew about it by the next day. As soon as he had bought the pub from Mr Niche, every man and his dog had turned up on his first night as owner landlord.

Old Mrs Compton walked through the door as he served a couple of walkers out viewing the sights.

'Usual, Mrs Compton?'

'Aye, lad,' she replied.

Brad poured out a glass of sherry. The bottle would sit on his shelf until Mrs Compton had drunk it all.

'Received a letter today, I did. Some cheeky whippersnapper wants to buy my cottage. I will leave that place only in a box, I tell you.' Her voice carried over the noise of the room.

'Just decline the offer and throw the letter in the bin,' Brad suggested calmly.

'What I want to know is why

someone wants to buy them all up. Mrs Longmire on the end has said she has had two offers now for her property,' she said, taking a sip from her drink before she put it down on the bar. 'Can you come over tomorrow, Brad? The lock on the back door is stiff.'

'Of course. Ten o'clock do you?' he asked, topping up the sherry glass as he spoke. 'You know everyone round here, don't you?'

'Aye, I was born and brought up in this village,' Mrs Compton replied.

'Mrs Howarth's niece — what is she like?'

Brad had been single for years, talent was thin on the ground and those women that were available were more like family than someone he could see himself spending the rest of his life with.

'She's a pretty young thing. Her eyes seem to glow each time she smiles. When she was a child, every time she walked into a room it would light up.'

Brad checked himself in the mirror.

He didn't consider himself to be every woman's dream man . . . Yes, he was tall and, at least in his humble opinion, he was presentable enough.

How vain can you get, Brad chastised himself.

'Brad?'

'Oh, sorry, Mrs Compton, I didn't mean to be rude.'

Everyone seemed up in arms about the proposed buy-out of the cottages, but as he lived in the pub, unless they built an eyesore across from him, he didn't really care.

'I thought we were having a conversation, young man. Obviously you have more important things on your mind.'

Mrs Compton wandered over to the fire and sat down, leaving Brad to wonder what on earth was getting people's backs up.

'Brad, perhaps I will see you in church next week?'

'Perhaps, vicar.'

The vicar, too, left him alone at the bar. It had quietened down now as most people were being brought their meals.

He needed a break himself. Could he leave Melissa in charge of the bar for a while until the rush had gone? It wasn't that he didn't trust her, but Sunday lunchtime was the busiest time for the Old Unicorn. Maybe he had just enough time to step outside for a breath of fresh air.

Brad wandered outside just as an old-style Rolls Royce pulled up outside the cottages.

He walked slowly and deliberately across the village green, just in time to see a beautiful girl with long, shapely legs climb out.

4

No Place Like Home

Gemma climbed out of the old Rolls Royce. Locking the door, she surveyed her surroundings.

It had been so long since she had been in Wythorne. The village green still looked as immaculate as she remembered. The old church stood just to her left and had the advantage of viewing the entire square. Several little shops stood at the furthest end away from her.

Gemma smiled to herself as she remembered the first time she had been able to leave her aunt's cottage and cross the square to go to the sweet shop. It had always been quite safe, with not many cars around and not many people, except on Sundays when it seemed the whole village descended on to the square.

The Old Unicorn was still standing.

Nothing seemed to have changed, but it was eerily quiet even though there were cars parked everywhere. She didn't believe in the atmosphere of place, but something felt wrong. The tranquillity was tinged with something else she couldn't put her finger on.

It was then she saw him — dressed in a pale blue shirt and jeans, heavy beige boots on his feet.

'Are you lost?'

Just the sound of his voice sent a shiver down her spine.

'Er, no . . . just moving in.'

'Sorry, how rude am I? I haven't introduced myself. I'm Brad — I run the Old Unicorn.' Brad held out his hand to her.

Gemma shook it nervously. He had her feeling like a giddy school girl.

'Gemma,' she offered, staring into his eyes as she spoke. They were the colour of toffee, but on closer inspection she saw they had golden flecks in them.

Get a grip, she said to herself. If she

wasn't careful she would end up a babbling idiot.

'Oh, you're Mrs Howarth's niece, aren't you?' Brad didn't really need her to answer him. Everyone had talked about her in the pub.

'Yes.'

He liked the way she tilted her head when she smiled.

'Do you want a hand?'

'Er, no . . . it's OK.'

'Honestly, it isn't a problem,' Brad urged. He really did want to help.

'There's only a few bags and boxes.'

'Well . . . if you're sure?'

'I am.'

'Perhaps you could come across to the pub later and I could fix you a bite to eat?' Brad suggested.

'Sure.' Gemma didn't want to turn him down for a second time. The offer of help had been welcome, but there wasn't really that much she couldn't do herself. Being on her own in a big city had made her fiercely independent and she was quite capable of doing this without a man around.

'See you about six, then?'

'Yes, six is fine.'

Gemma watched Brad walk across the green and into the pub.

The drive had made her weary, but the boxes and bags couldn't get up and walk into the house on their own.

Slowly walking up two stone steps into the garden, she stopped and listened. Silence. The only sound she could hear was birdsong — so different to the sounds she was used to. No cars speeding, horns or even shouts from passers-by.

Gemma couldn't believe she had forgotten just how pretty Wythorne was or how calming for the soul.

She paused for a moment, rummaging around in her handbag for the keys. They were extremely old and rusty, and she doubted that they would even work.

To her surprise, the key slipped effortlessly into the lock without any problems. The heavy oak door with its iron fittings reminded her of the church door just across the way.

Inside the cottage nothing had changed, except for the fact that her aunt had always kept the cottage as neat as a new pin, and now thick dust covered all the surfaces. The entire house would need a deep clean.

Walking upstairs, Gemma headed to her old bedroom, pushing open the door to see the familiar purple walls and plush velvet curtains.

Gemma wasn't surprised to see that her room had stayed the same. Flinging open the curtains and the sash window to air the room, a wave of sadness washed over her. Why hadn't she come back sooner whilst her aunt was still here?

After she had deposited all her things in all the right rooms, she would need to decide on a plan of action. As long as she had a bed to sleep on and milk for a cup of tea in the morning she would be fine.

Locking the house back up, she headed across the road to the village shop cum post office.

Gemma looked through the window and saw several women already standing around the counter chatting away to each other.

The bell tinkled as she walked inside, and everyone stopped to see who had just come in.

'Oh, it's little Gemma, isn't it? I'd recognise you anywhere.'

The woman who spoke was all dressed in black, but her long blonde hair was tied into a messy ponytail.

'Yes, it is.' Gemma nodded. 'I'm sorry, do I know you?'

'Oh, I'm Edith, your aunt's old next door neighbour — before I moved, of course.'

'I'm sorry. I didn't recognise you.' Gemma decided it would be impolite of her to say she didn't remember her at all.

'Have you come to see the house before you sell up?'

Gemma looked at Edith incredulously.

'Sell up? Where on earth did you get that idea from?'

'Well, we all did,' Edith replied.

Gemma watched Edith turn to her friends to back up her statement and they all duly nodded.

'I have received an offer, but I am turning it down.' Gemma looked at their blank faces. 'What on earth is going on?'

'Some property developer wants to buy the cottages and put a factory on the site.' The speaker was an elderly lady wearing a pink shawl and tweed skirt.

'A factory in the middle of Wythorne? Tell me you're joking.' Gemma was aghast.

'No, it's true. All of us have had offers. Nasty threatening letters, too.' Edith took over talking again. Gemma got the distinct impression she was the spokesperson for the group.

'Gemma, why don't you come to the women's group over at the church later?'

'I don't understand.' Gemma frowned. 'If you moved, then how come you've received a threatening letter?'

'Didn't I say? I came back to live in the cottage. I had to move because I got a job in Manchester and when I retired I moved back home.'

Suddenly Judy Garland's voice popped into Gemma's head.

'There's no place like home,' it chanted.

'So, what about the women's meeting? We're discussing the May Day fete and bake off,' the woman in the tweed skirt said.

'You still do the May Day celebrations?' Gemma hadn't seen one of those for years. She remembered dressing up in a neighbour's pink bridesmaid's dress for a Victorian-themed one.

'Oh, yes. We now have a craft competition, bake off and, of course, the contest for the best garden in the village. As you know, at our autumn fete we have the best vegetable instead of the garden.'

Gemma hadn't expected to do anything other than move back to Wythorne, lick her wounds and write another cookbook.

She would need a full-time job, too. Maybe she could get one at the local school in the kitchen, something to keep in with cooking.

'Sure, what time do you meet?' Gemma asked rather abruptly.

'Seven-thirty in the church.'

'OK, I'll see you then.' Gemma looked at her watch. It was already half-past five and Brad was expecting her over at the pub shortly.

Gemma walked out of the shop then returned almost immediately. She had forgotten to get the milk she had gone in for.

'Back so soon?' a middle-aged woman with shoulder-length brown hair and beady eyes addressed her.

'Yes, I would forget my head if it wasn't screwed on.' Gemma held up the carton of milk.

'You do know there is a milkman if

you want a pint on your doorstep?'

'No, I didn't. Have you got the phone number and I'll give him a call?'

Gemma thought that the woman was a bit too harsh in the way she was speaking to her. For some reason the woman behind the counter reminded her of a sneaky, twitchy rat.

'Sorry, I didn't catch your name,' Gemma added.

'Sorry, I'm Margaret, my boyfriend Thomas runs the baker's at the end of the street. His batch loafs are just delicious.'

Gemma paid for the milk and left the shop as quickly as possible. The women from the church had now congregated on the pavement outside, huddled together having a mothers' meeting.

5

Someone to Trust

Night was slowly creeping in as Gemma watched the sun sinking behind Pendle Hill. It was a shame that the famous witch trials were over — there were a few of the villagers she would like to throw in Lancaster Jail.

Entering the pub, she was surprised by how busy it was. The old snug door was closed, but the laughter coming from inside let everyone know there was a noisy game of darts or dominoes going on. Gemma smiled. Nothing much changes, she thought.

All the stools by the bar had been taken so she would have to wait her turn.

'Hey, Gemma!' Brad hollered to her, raising his hand above the sea of heads surrounding him. 'I reserved a table for you by the fire. Go and sit down and I'll be over in a minute.'

It was nice to see that someone was true to his word. Gemma did as she was bid and walked to the designated table.

People stared at her as she walked past them. Let them stare, her Auntie Clara would have said. They must not have anything interesting going on in their lives.

Gemma pulled out her chair and sat down. Picking up a beer mat, she placed it at the edge of the table and began flipping it. Old habits die hard — after all, she would do this whenever she had been bored waiting for food when she was younger.

Brad seemed to have a smile and a chat with everyone who came to buy a drink. He was handsome in a kindly sort of way, and softly spoken. Perfect — perhaps too perfect, if that was possible. At least it was a different attitude than the men in the city had. All they cared about was how much money they had or what sort of cars they drove around in.

Brad finally sauntered over to her table.

'I can do anything you want. There's a shepherd's pie with your name on it, or beef stew and dumplings.'

Gemma contemplated what to have. They both sounded good.

'Any chance I can have a bit of both?'

OK, so she would come across as greedy, but she hadn't eaten since this morning and if Edith expected her over at the church in an hour it would be late by the time she got anything.

As if on cue her belly rumbled.

'Of course you can. Be right back,' Brad replied.

She watched him walk towards the kitchen but lost sight of him as he disappeared down the corridor and felt a bit disappointed.

No, Gemma! She shook her head. You're not here to find a relationship.

She didn't want to wait for ages to be fed, but she didn't need to panic. Brad soon came back carrying a plate loaded with shepherd's pie and beef stew.

Gemma thanked him before she started on her meal. Brad sat down across from her, which was unnerving as he didn't speak.

'You can talk to me. I don't bite, you know.' She smiled.

'Yes, but you're from the city — used to the bright lights,' Brad said hesitantly.

'I came from Wythorne, same as you.'

'Oh, I'm not from Wythorne. I come from Hunswood originally, just a few miles out of the village.'

Gemma looked at him. Hunswood village was even smaller than her own, but the woods, she had to admit, were second to none.

'I remember Aunt Clara and I often went mushroom-picking in the woods. Stuffed mushroom was her favourite, but she would always say that nothing could beat fresh mushrooms with a full English breakfast.'

Brad chuckled.

'I still do go and pick mushrooms and use them in some of my recipes.'

'I hope you take a book with you, so you know which mushrooms are safe,' Gemma replied, before taking another fork full of her food.

'Of course. I wouldn't want to poison anyone.'

'I've heard of many unfortunate mishaps happening to people who picked their own mushrooms.' Gemma sighed heavily. It had been a stupid thing to do, ordering two dishes for her tea.

'I have to ask — what are you going to do with the house?'

Well, that was straight to the point, she thought.

'What on earth has got everyone so rattled?' she asked rather too sharply. 'Just because someone wants to buy the cottages doesn't mean the owners have to sell them.'

'It's not just that they have received offers, other things have been happening.' Brad fell silent and Gemma got the impression that he wanted to say more but wouldn't. Even though she had grown up in Wythorne, she was still a stranger around here, and someone to be eyed with suspicion.

'I've got to get back to the bar,' Brad finally said. 'The meal's on the house.'

'No — please, let me pay.'

'It's fine, honestly. Look, why don't I come around tomorrow and give you a hand sorting things out?'

Gemma smiled.

'That would be great. Tonight I'm off to the women's group at the church.' She had no enthusiasm for it — an early night and a decent night's rest was what she really wanted.

'Well, I can see the May Day bake off will be fun this year. The chef behind 'Queenie's Quick Meals' is going to get first place.' Brad let out a huge belly laugh, but Gemma had no idea why it was so funny, or even if she could trust someone she had only just met.

'How did you know the name of the show?'

'They have all been talking about the show.'

Gemma finished her ale and headed over to the church, trepidation filling her entire being.

6

Sinister Message

Gemma stepped out into the wintry night air. The pub car park was still as full as it had been earlier, even though there didn't seem to have been many people in the Old Unicorn. Looking across the road to the church, she could see the lights were on, illuminating the beautiful stained-glass windows depicting saints and Bible scenes.

The main doors were fastened open and one of the glass inner doors was held open by a huge wooden stopper. Not since she had been younger had she stepped through the ornate archway and into the church itself.

Gemma heard muffled voices. People must have arrived for the women's group already.

She looked at the stairs to her left.

The entire upper floor looked to be in complete darkness and had a very eerie feel to it. Gemma remembered many a happy Friday night up there learning disco dancing, and then Sunday school on Sundays until she had been old enough to move downstairs.

The idea of walking into a room full of strangers scared her a little, even though she had met a few of them briefly at the shop. They had all seemed to eye her with suspicion and that unnerved her more than anything.

One voice seemed louder than anyone else's and Gemma recognised it as Edith's.

Gemma took her time walking the short distance to the room in front of her. What had possessed her to agree to this in the first place?

The cancellation of 'Queenie's Quick Meals' was still uppermost in her mind. Although the show was named after the presenter, Gemma was the brains behind it, and she was always behind the scenes producing the food whilst someone else took all the credit for her hard work. She was angry at the television station not only for that, but for the fact that she had lost her job and flat.

Moving back to her home village hadn't been a part of her life plan. Her first night back and she was going to be spending it discussing a bake off for a group of village ladies.

Gemma opened the door, which squeaked as she did so. There was only one table being used, but the hatch to the kitchen was open.

One lady with strawberry blonde hair held a pen and paper as if her life depended on it. Everyone stared at Gemma, but then turned back and continued their conversations as before. It was several minutes before Edith called the meeting to order.

Gemma still stood uncertainly.

'Gemma, come and sit down,' Edith said to her.

Gemma complied and took the only available seat between Edith and the lady with the pen.

'Right, girls, we need to discuss the bake off,' Edith said authoritatively.

The lady with the pen looked at Gemma.

'Oh, you're Mrs Howarth's niece, aren't you?' It was more a statement of fact than a question.

'Yes, I am. Sorry, what's your name?'

'I'm Mrs Longmire, dear. I live at the end of the cottages.' She smiled in a friendly way.

On the other hand, Edith looked at everyone with daggers in her eyes. She obviously wanted to start the meeting, and no-one was paying the least attention to her.

'Right . . . this year's May Day festival will start with the crowning of the May Queen. A parade through Wythorne and a small church service afterwards, then the festivities will start. Any objections?'

Gemma looked around the room, but everyone stayed silent, so Edith continued her speech.

'We will have stalls of various types on the village green and here in the church hall; the bake off entries and the craft stalls will be upstairs.'

'What sort of stalls?' Gemma asked.

'The usual — white elephant, tombola, books. Well, you know the sort of thing,' Edith piped up.

'OK, I was just asking.' That sounded harsher than Gemma had intended.

Mrs Longmire wrote down in neat writing everything that was said.

'Now, does anyone have any suggestions as to the type of food stalls we should have?'

'Perhaps Mrs Compton could make her famous home-made jams and chutneys and sell them alongside Thomas's baked goods.'

Mrs Compton, Gemma presumed, nodded her agreement. Nothing had been said about why Gemma was here. It seemed they had everything under control.

'I presume you will be entering again, Mrs Withenshaw?'

'Of course.'

Gemma didn't like the way Mrs Withenshaw looked around the room, but kept quiet. She didn't feel able to air her concerns.

'How about we celebrate the British Isles through our cakes and puddings?' It was the first time Gemma had spoken up so far.

'Does anyone else have any ideas?' Edith looked around the room.

'How about the old-fashioned school pudding bake off? We could have sticky toffee pudding?'

'So, we have two options for our bake off theme. Can anyone think of anything else?'

Mrs Longmire looked at the group and then suggested main meals.

'No, Mrs Longmire, it is a bake off, which means we need to make some sort of puddings,' Edith replied kindly. 'OK, we will vote. Put your hand up if you agree with Gemma's suggestion of cakes from around the British Isles?'

Several hands went up. Gemma

wasn't sure whose hand belonged to whom.

'And who is for the school puddings idea?'

Gemma saw Edith check the hands. There were much fewer for that idea than her own and it didn't take a genius to figure out she had won.

'I believe Gemma's idea wins. I'm sorry, Mrs Miller, but how about we do your idea for the harvest festival?'

Gemma couldn't help but smile and Mrs Miller, in her mismatched outfit, was smiling, too.

The women around the table muttered to the person next to them, but surprisingly it was Mrs Compton who spoke first.

'I think that it is a great idea.'

It was then everyone agreed to the plan.

'I will get our Steve to do all the printing and ask the vicar to announce it during the church service.' Edith spoke, silencing the whole room.

'Well, that seems to be the bake off

sorted. I am looking forward to this year's festival,' Edith announced.

Mrs Withenshaw looked directly at Gemma.

'I don't understand why Miss Howarth's niece should be here and involved in matters which have nothing to do with her.'

Mrs Compton just stared at her.

'Mrs Withenshaw, Gemma was born and brought up here. She has just as much right to be here as us.'

'I'm sorry, I beg to differ, Mrs Compton.'

Gemma watched the exchange and thought that if looks could kill she would be dead. She had only just met Mrs Withenshaw, but already she didn't like her. There was something seriously wrong with that woman.

If she thought it was all right to attack a stranger for no reason and whenever she felt like it, she had another think coming. Nobody else was as nasty as her. Perhaps Mrs Withenshaw should get on her broom and fly away like the Lancashire witches.

Gemma knew in that moment, and for whatever reason, old Mrs Withenshaw disliked her and her aunt. Perhaps this woman could, and would, cause trouble. Gemma made her mind up to keep an eye on her.

'Look, it's late. Why don't we call it a night?' Mrs Compton looked sympathetically at Gemma. 'I will walk back to the cottages with you as it's getting dark.'

'Of course, Mrs Compton.' Gemma stood up and waited whilst her escort said goodbye to her friends.

Gemma received a few cursory nods. Other than Mrs Compton, only Edith said goodbye to her in a friendly manner. Mrs Miller was, Gemma presumed, still smarting at the thought her idea hadn't been well received. Mrs Compton was still saying her farewells, but Gemma was feeling an urgent need to run out of there.

'Come on, dear.' Mrs Compton slid her arm through Gemma's. 'You don't mind walking an old woman home, do you?'

'Of course not, Mrs Compton.'

'Oh, enough with the 'Mrs' malarkey. Call me Daisy — your aunt and I were great friends.'

'If you're certain, then I will.' It was nice to be accepted by only the second person in this village.

Gemma felt a bit guilty. It wasn't that bad, but the people here had their own agenda and it was obvious they didn't appreciate strangers — not ones who had left and returned for unknown reasons, at least as far as they were concerned.

'Why don't you come in for a cup of tea and perhaps some toast and marmalade?' Daisy suggested.

'Marmalade?'

'Oh, yes,' Daisy said animatedly. 'I found a great recipe for Maggie's Dundee marmalade. I intend to sell it at the fete, but I need a guinea pig and you're it.'

Gemma held back her laughter.

'Why don't you call it Daisy's marmalade?'

'No, I couldn't do that. It is someone else's recipe, so their name will be on the labels. Maggie is an acquaintance of mine and someone who went above and beyond for me on more than one occasion.'

Gemma was a tad jealous. None of her homemade jams and marmalade ever set properly, so she would always buy chutneys or jams for the recipes she did for the show.

As they reached Daisy's cottage they heard voices behind them as the other women came out of the church.

'Come on in quick; it's too cold to be standing out here. To be honest, Gemma, I've had enough of those cronies for one day,' Daisy urged.

This time Gemma laughed out loud.

'I thought they were your friends.'

'They are — all except Mrs Withenshaw — she is nobody's friend but her own. She just hates to be beaten at anything.'

Gemma waited patiently until Daisy had opened her front door. Crisp lines and modern furniture offset the flowery wallpaper, which was not at all what she expected to see.

A large fireguard protected the room from any rogue sparks. Several portraits adorned the walls that Gemma presumed to be of family members.

'Come into the kitchen.' Mrs Compton led the way through the narrow passageway. It looked as though she had had a downstairs bathroom installed, as the passageway into her aunt Clara's kitchen was much larger.

'Would you like me to do anything?'

'Yes, dear. Just turn the gas on and put the kettle on the hob for me, please, whilst I get the cups and do the bread and marmalade.'

Gemma did as she was asked. There was something strangely comforting about the whistling of a kettle.

Once the kettle began to sing, she poured the water into the cups and brewed the tea. There was a teapot on the table which seemed to be for decorative purposes only.

Mrs Compton carried two plates of thick white bread covered in marmalade over to the table, whilst Gemma carried the tea. After looking at the plates an idea hit Gemma, and she was sure it would be a winner at the fete.

'Are you going to bottle it?'

'Oh, yes, my dear. I have Steve print out all the labels for me — at cost, of course — then I always give him a few jars of whatever he likes to give to his wife.'

'That's very nice of you, Mrs Compton.'

It always amazed Gemma that people of a certain age always got what they wanted in the way they wanted.

'I've told you — enough of the 'Mrs' stuff.'

'I'm sorry, I will have to remember. I'm jealous because I can never get my jams to set.'

'Oh, I can help you.' Daisy's face lit up, 'You know it's so nice to have a young 'un around the place. How about you show me how to make your famous Battenberg cake? Clara raved about it.'

'It's a deal.' Gemma smiled. 'Have you had any of these letters asking you to sell your house?'

'I wouldn't use the word 'asking', if I were you.' Daisy stood and went over to her bureau, the only old-fashioned piece in the place, and started rummaging through the top drawers.

'I received this the other day,' she said, holding a paper out to Gemma.

Gemma looked at the typewritten letter.

'Mrs Compton,' Gemma read aloud, although she wasn't sure why. 'Your house is about to be condemned and if I were you I would get out while you can before your house falls down around you. Sell to me, or else.'

7

Dear Diary . . .

'That is a very threatening letter. Have you gone to the police?' Gemma was startled at the wording. She could only imagine what the rest of the letters said.

'No, I just put them in the drawer and ignore them.'

'What do you mean you ignore them? How many have you had?'

'Oh, about six or seven. They're in the bureau over there. Help yourself.'

Gemma hesitated.

'Go on, Gemma. Do what you are told and check.' Daisy laughed. 'You know just how much you're like Clara, don't you?'

'I guess I am. I can't believe she's gone.'

'No, neither can I. She was as strong as an ox.'

Gemma stared at the bureau and opened the drawer, taking a handful of letters fastened by an elastic band. There must have been seven or eight of them.

'You know what's strange?' Gemma said slowly. 'Aunt Clara wasn't sick. She came down to see me a few weeks before she died and we did the whole tourist thing. You know — Buckingham Palace, Madame Tussauds, the whole works.'

'I'd love to go to London,' Daisy replied.

'I will have to take you there sometime.' Gemma was serious in her offer, but she caught the 'I don't think you mean it' look from Daisy.

'Don't worry about me.' Daisy's face fell. 'Clara was my closest friend. Since my husband died, I've only had her and the other ladies who go to the church.'

'Don't you have children?'

'No, we were never blessed that way.'

Gemma felt awful to think Daisy was

alone in the world. She sat back down at the kitchen table.

'Do these letters all say the same thing?'

'Yes, all the same as the one you have already read.'

Gemma took her empty plate and cup over to the sink.

'I wonder if everyone else's letters were the same as this one?'

'Oh, just leave the dishes. I will do them after.'

Gemma was getting slightly irritated by Daisy's apparently casual attitude to it all.

'Why isn't this letter written on headed notepaper?' Gemma asked.

'Oh, I don't know, dear. Most of the letters are hand delivered. I can't afford a surveyor to look at the cottage and see if it will fall down around my ears,' Daisy replied sadly.

Gemma paced around the kitchen. This wasn't right. Most people had received threatening letters trying to get them to sell up. This man, whoever he was, had got the people frightened. After all, you couldn't put a factory in the middle of a village, but that was what they all believed.

Gemma didn't have much money, either, but perhaps one of the surveying students from the local college would do it for a reasonable price. Their findings wouldn't be legally binding, but at least she and her new neighbours would have a better idea about everything.

'Has the village council done anything?' Gemma asked.

'They've said there is nothing they can do if people decide to sell their houses.' Daisy looked despondent.

'Well, they're not getting my cottage, no matter what threats they try to make.' Gemma squeezed the old lady's hand. 'We will beat them. I promise.'

Daisy stayed quiet and Gemma assumed that she was considering selling.

'How can we beat them?' Daisy asked.

'I'm not sure yet, Daisy, but we will. I've promised you.'

'You're welcome around here any time you like.' Daisy seemed hopeful and Gemma thought she was someone that she would really like to spend time with.

'I'd best get home. It's getting late and I don't seem to have stopped since I arrived from London.' Gemma picked up her jacket.

'No, you get away, lass. Call tomorrow if you like. I will be in.'

Gemma thanked Daisy for the tea, and with the promise of seeing her the following day, she wandered home.

She had a lot to think about and a lot of things to sort out in the house. She knew from the short space of time she had spent in Clara's cottage that all the windows would need replacing and some of the brickwork could do with re-pointing.

* * *

Taking out the large key to her aunt's house, Gemma paused when she heard someone speak. It was very faint, but she was almost certain she heard Mrs Miller's name mentioned but nothing else.

Shrugging it off, Gemma went inside and made sure to double bolt the front door. Hurrying through to the kitchen, she made sure that the back door was also securely locked.

Her new home was decorated much differently from the way Daisy had done hers. Most of Aunt Clara's furnishings were old-fashioned chintz patterns and net curtains that had yellowed with age. It all needed redecorating, but Gemma hadn't much money to do everything that needed done.

Even her car had been given to her by Aunt Clara. Her aunt no longer used it and that model of Rolls Royce wasn't made any more.

All Aunt Clara's trophies stood on the mantelpiece, except for the one she had won last year which still stood on the small table by her armchair.

Gemma switched out the lights and headed upstairs. With each step she took, the wooden stairs creaked and groaned.

I'll need to get a carpet down here, she decided. More money to pay out — wonderful!

Instead of turning right to her bedroom, she turned to her left and headed into her aunt's bedroom. The old-fashioned counterpane lay neatly folded at the bottom of her bed. A silver trunk sat on the floor, the tiny key still in the lock.

Part of her wanted to head to bed, but the other wanted to see what secrets her aunt had kept in the little trunk.

Spurred on by the thoughts of hand-embroidered hankies, or perhaps letters of love, Gemma walked slowly towards the chest. Kneeling, she carefully lifted the lid on the trunk. It was unlocked and at the very top was an old book.

Gemma carefully lifted it out and found it was her aunt's diary. Opening it to the first page, she began to read.

'Our Gemma has gone off to start a new life in London working for a TV show. I'm going to miss her terribly, but I have said that I will come down for visits. Her parents would be so proud of what she has become. It's a shame her mother is no longer here to see it.

'Over the next few weeks I need to prepare my cake for the bake off. Mrs Withenshaw is getting extremely nasty as one more win for me will mean we will be neck and neck. Some of her latest creations haven't gone down as well as in years gone by. Mrs Miller has caught up on the trophy front, too, and that didn't make that old battle-axe Withenshaw happy, but I was so proud of Mrs Miller.'

Gemma closed the book. It had been started a few months before the May Day fete, the last entry being on the day Aunt Clara died.

There would be more time to read

the diary later. Now she needed to go to bed, but something kept nagging at her, twisting her insides.

Something in Gemma's subconscious told her to be careful — but of what? She would have to wait and see what would happen.

8

Caught in a Fix

Gemma awoke before sunrise, having spent half the night tossing and turning due to the wind howling through gaps in the windows and rain dripping down from the ceiling on to the stairs all through the night. She had had to go in search of a bucket to catch the rainwater. Consequently she was feeling less than refreshed and not in the best of moods.

The house was cold even though the heating was supposedly turned up high. Gemma had to do something — she couldn't leave things the way they were. Maybe she could give the college a ring to see if some of the students would like to come out and fix the house cheaply as part of their course. Either that or she would have to find a local tradesman who wouldn't charge her a fortune.

It wasn't just the inside of the cottage that needed redecoration, but also the outside needed a lot of work, probably more than she could afford at the moment.

Just as Gemma was debating on a plan of action the doorbell rang — a strident rendition of the 'Black Beauty' theme song.

Another thing I need to fix, she thought to herself.

Who would come around at this time in the morning? Gemma wasn't in any mood to entertain. Then suddenly a horrid thought crossed her mind. What if there was something wrong with Mrs Compton?

Gemma dashed to the door, unlocking it as quickly as possible, and was relieved to see her fears were unfounded.

'Brad! Do you have any idea what time it is?'

The landlord of the pub stood before

her, tray in hand.

'I thought you might be hungry.'

'Seriously? I'm not exactly in the mood for guests.'

'Come on, Gemma, I know you haven't been to the supermarket. Your car hasn't moved since you got here.

She felt guilty. Brad was just being kind.

'I'm sorry, I guess you had better come in.' Gemma moved to one side.

'You look shattered,' Brad remarked as he stepped over the threshold into the cottage.

'So would you be if you had spent half the night trying to stop water pouring into your house.' Gemma led him towards the kitchen.

Gemma wasn't happy to see Brad this morning. Not that he had done anything wrong, it was just that she was always grumpy until she'd had at least three cups of tea.

Gemma caught the look of concern on Brad's face.

'Is there anything I can help you

with?' he asked.

'Let me put the kettle on.'

'No, I'll do it while you eat your breakfast before it goes cold.'

Gemma did as she was asked and sat at the old oak table. Lifting the silver lid carefully from the plate, she was surprised to see a full cooked English breakfast complete with mushrooms.

'Handpicked mushrooms?'

'Oh, yes. Can't beat them.'

As Gemma tucked into her full breakfast she was grateful to Brad for bringing it round. He was showing kindness to a stranger — something very rare in this day and age.

'Gemma, do you want me to have a look at the roof for you? I have a ladder over at the Old Unicorn.'

The way he smiled at her made Gemma shiver. Brad was a handsome man and didn't seem to have a bad bone in his body. He was the sort of man she liked, but there was no way he would be interested in someone like her.

After all, her arrival in Wythorne seemed to have the whole village's backs up. Gemma had no idea why. It wasn't as though she was a total stranger, but if people remembered her living there they weren't saying anything.

'That would be great, but I wouldn't want you to hurt yourself on my account.' The roof would be wet and slippery from all the rain during the night.

'Don't worry about me. I will be perfectly safe.'

Brad oozed confidence. It was a shame that Gemma didn't share his confidence, but she had little choice with no money and a house that needed renovating inside and out.

'Brad, how come you want to help me?' she asked quietly.

'I liked your aunt and feel I need to look after the most important person in her life.' When Brad smiled he showed all his white teeth and his eyes sparkled with delight.

‘I was?’ she said incredulously.

‘Of course, the way she used to talk about you and your show. She was so proud of you.’

Tears fell silently down Gemma’s cheeks, remembering her aunt’s cheeky smile and constant nudges to have a snack.

‘Hey, are you OK?’

‘Yes. Sorry, I was just remembering something.’

Gemma finished up her breakfast and put her plate in the sink.

‘That was delicious, thank you. I really needed that.’

‘You’re welcome. Just call it Brad’s meals on wheels.’ They both laughed, lightening the mood between them.

‘So, what can you tell me about some of the people here?’ Gemma realised how that sounded, but she couldn’t recall any of the people here in the village. Some were vaguely familiar, but others she had no recollection of at all. Even when she had lived in the village she hadn’t bothered with many people, and now she couldn't remember why.

'Mrs Miller is a nice lady, and the reverend is always happy to help anyone. He is the first one to prop up the bar after Sunday service. Mrs Withenshaw is a bit of a one — everything must be done her way or no way. And, of course, you have Mrs Longmire, an ex-English teacher at the old boys' grammar school.'

'I remember Mrs Longmire. She was always bringing books around to Aunt Clara's for me to read.'

Brad smiled at her, a smile that reached his eyes.

'Look, Brad, while you're here, do you know anything about central heating? The house is freezing.'

'Let me have a look. Where's your boiler?' Brad stood up and wandered around the room.

'It's in the larder, but why anyone would put a boiler in the larder is beyond me.'

Gemma caught him looking around.

'I know it all needs decorating.'

She would leave her aunt's bedroom the way it was, perhaps just give the skirting boards and door frame a fresh lick of paint. For some reason it would upset her too much to change the house beyond any recognition.

The settees were really old, but the sort that you could happily curl up in with a good book and a hot chocolate on cold Lancashire nights.

'I can help you decorate. I have white gloss and some emulsion in the cellar over at the pub.'

'Let me know how much I owe you for the paint.'

Brad put his hand up.

'You don't owe me anything.'

'Then I guess I will owe you a meal by the time we have finished.' Gemma looked up at him, trying to read what he was thinking, but his mask was back in place.

Gemma showed him the boiler and dug out a few screwdrivers she'd found in the bottom of the kitchen drawer. If this was the extent of her aunt's tool box then she wouldn't get very far at all.

Just opening the boiler was enough to see what was wrong with it. By the looks of it, the whole boiler looked rusted and dead. Gemma was no electrician or gas expert, but the insides didn't look bright and sparkling — more like a crushed raspberry.

'This needs replacing. It's gone completely.' Brad waved the screwdriver around inside the boiler.

'I have a friend of a friend who can help with the boiler. He owes me a favour.'

Gemma stifled a laugh.

'Some guy you met down the pub?'

Brad laughed with her.

'Oh, very witty. Someone certainly has cheered up, haven't they?'

'Must be the company I've started to keep. This boiler is going to cost a lot, isn't it?'

'Just the price of the boiler — as long as you don't need new pipes. If you do the cost will sky rocket.'

'Wonderful! Can things get any worse after last night?' Gemma replied almost absentmindedly.

'Why? What happened last night?'

'You know I was invited to the church women's group?' Gemma waited for any sense of acknowledgment, but when she received none she carried on regardless. 'Well, Mrs Withenshaw was rather nasty and made it perfectly clear I wasn't welcome at the meeting,' she replied, leaning on the door frame. 'Whatever her problem is, I wish she would keep it to herself.'

'She's always like that. Always assumes she is better than anyone else. Her husband's a truck driver and away an awful lot.' Brad could sympathise with Gemma as anyone on the wrong side of Mrs Withenshaw usually found themselves as outcasts in the community. He had known people who had been threatened by her son if they had crossed her.

'Well, I think it's rude and totally out

of order.' Gemma folded her arms angrily. 'What happened to people being nice to each other?'

'I don't know. She is one of these that if you have had success in writing an article for the local paper, she has written for 'The Times'. Our dear Mrs Withenshaw is like that.'

'There's plenty of people like that in London. I wish when people are your friends they are real friends and not happy to stab you in the back just because they think they are better than you.'

Brad frowned.

'It's certainly not like it used to be, that's for sure.' He couldn't tell Gemma — or could he? — that Mrs Withenshaw tried owning everyone and everything in the village. Surely no harm would come to Gemma if he kept her in the dark.

'There's something else bothering you. You can tell me,' he urged.

'Well, it's something I was thinking about last night. My aunt's death was strange. It was odd that she died so suddenly.'

Brad stared intently at Gemma before answering.

'Grief does strange things to people,' he said gently.

'I guess.' But Gemma wasn't convinced that was all it was. 'Look, I need to go around the house and make lists of everything that needs fixing or replacing. I don't suppose you want to help?'

'Sure, but I have to open the pub at twelve.'

Grabbing his hand, Gemma dragged him into the living-room.

'We'll start in here.'

Armed only with notebook and pen, Brad pointed to the ceiling rose and a large crack permeating from it.

'Yes, that needs sorting. Do you think there are any problems with subsidence?' Gemma asked.

'No, I don't think so. There's nothing on the walls outside to suggest that,' Brad said as he wandered over to the fireplace. 'I'd get this checked out, too, whilst you're about it.'

'Yes, the last thing I need to do is get carbon monoxide poisoning.' Gemma scribbled notes as they went through each room of the cottage. The list of things to do was growing with two sets of eyes looking into every nook and cranny of the house.

'This lot is going to cost me a fortune.' Gemma sighed sadly.

'I have a few friends in the building trade,' Brad told her. 'They owe me a few favours, and if you knock up one of your famous dinners, I'm sure that they would do it for materials only.'

'Do you really think so?'

Brad just smiled in reply. At least he would get to spend more time with her. He'd even thought of offering her a job at the pub to earn some money.

'There's the fete in three days. How about we leave it until after that and we can talk again?' Gemma said.

They wandered back into the kitchen and Gemma went to put the kettle on.

'Why after the fete? What are you cooking up, Ms Howarth?'

'I'm thinking of entering, but don't tell anyone.' Gemma realised that she shouldn't really have said anything. After all, he could tell the whole village in the space of two minutes over at the Old Unicorn.

'I won't say anything and you're lucky I'm not judging that this year — only the homemade ale competition.'

'I didn't realise that was part of the programme.'

'It's a late addition really. The money raised from it will go to the local hospice.'

9

The Girl of his Dreams

By the time Gemma and Brad had finished listing everything that needed to be done to the cottage it was nearly 11.30. Brad took a quick look at his watch.

'I will have to go soon, Gem.' He hoped that Gemma wouldn't notice his slip of shortening her name, and if she did that she wouldn't pull him up on it.

'Yes, OK. I might pop into the pub for my tea. Can I ask you something?'

'Fire away.'

'What do you know about this property developer? Although she pretends to make light of it, I can tell Mrs Compton is extremely worried.'

'I don't know much more than you, except that someone wants to buy all the cottages and put a factory there, or at least that is what everyone is saying. Planning permission would be hard to get for something like that.' Brad walked over to the sink to wash his hands.

Brad was touched by the concern Gemma was showing her new neighbours. She had been here such a short time but had already made an impression on him.

After seeing her last night in the pub, he hadn't thought of anything else but Gemma all night. She had filled his dreams. He had noticed the way she spoke kindly to everyone, but he was just as sure that she could give as good as she got.

'Why did you move back — if you don't mind me asking?' Brad was trying not to be nosy, but he couldn't help being curious.

'It's a long story,' Gemma said sadly.

'I have all the time in the world,' Brad said. 'Well, OK, not quite — about ten minutes.'

Gemma laughed.

'Well, as you know I was an assistant on a TV show.' Gemma jumped up and sat on the worktop. 'I did all the baking, prep work — you name it, although I didn't get any of the credit.'

Brad gave her a wry smile.

The marble counter was cold, so Gemma shuffled around as she went on.

'The bosses at the studio told me they were cancelling the show. I no longer had a job or a flat, as that belonged to the studio.'

'So, without a job at the studio you wouldn't have a home, either. That seems totally wrong. Wasn't there anything you could do?'

'Nope. I was glad Aunt Clara left me the cottage, but I would rather have a job and have her back with me,' Gemma answered sadly.

Brad gave her a sympathetic look but Gemma shrugged. She didn't need sympathy from Brad — in fact, she didn't need it from anyone.

She had known what accepting the

flat would mean when she'd taken the job. Sometimes things worked out to your advantage and at other times you lost.

Brad picked up his abandoned cup and drank the last dregs of coffee.

'So, what did you do at the studio, then?'

'What didn't I do, don't you mean?'

Everyone here seems to think I'm some big star, Gemma couldn't help thinking.

'I did the baking,' she continued.

'Coming up with recipes and getting all the ingredients ready for the star of the show. I had to make it look like she had done everything, when all she actually did was look good on screen.' Gemma's foot banged on the cupboard in annoyance.

'That doesn't sound good.' There wasn't a lot he could say in defence of the studio, but the look of anger on Gemma's face told him he would be best to keep quiet. 'I'd better get back over to the pub. I'll come back at closing time and give you a hand if you want to start painting.'

'Sure, that would be great, thanks. Don't forget, though, that you may be feeding me yet.' Gemma jumped down from the counter. 'I need to get this roof sorted out. Thanks for breakfast, it was delicious.'

* * *

Brad said his goodbyes and left Gemma alone in the kitchen. She decided to phone the college just to see if the students could come and do a survey on the whole row of cottages. It would help by putting the other residents' minds at rest, especially Daisy's and Mrs Longmire's.

Maybe she could walk around the whole building and see if she could see a big crack in the brick work. If there wasn't then it might be in a place that she wouldn't be able to reach without a ladder. Then maybe she could read a bit of her aunt's diary or see how Mrs Compton was.

Gemma needed a trip out to see if she could get some supplies, but the last thing she wanted was to see Mrs Withenshaw.

Bread, she needed some bread. She could nip across the road and visit Thomas's shop. She had yet to meet Margaret's fiancé. That would be interesting, and maybe he also sold some nice buns for when she couldn't be bothered to bake for herself.

First, she needed to make that phone call to the college. Gemma wandered into the hallway where the phone sat on a little table at the base of the stairs — not the most convenient place to have it. She would need to have an extension put in or a cordless phone and the base unit here.

It seemed as though there was so much she needed to do and so much that needed replacing, and money was going to be a big issue. The fact was that she had very little — only the amount the studio had given her for her last wage packet and the small legacy from her aunt which she was trying to hang on to for as long as possible.

After making several calls to roofers for quotes, Gemma finally accepted one from a tradesman who could come later in the day to erect scaffolding and put a sheet of tarpaulin down to stop any rain from getting in if it rained during the night. He could start work properly tomorrow. Gemma had just enough money to cover it.

What she needed was a job — and quick. Maybe Brad needed bar staff at the Old Unicorn. She would ask him later in the day when she saw him again.

The man in charge of surveying said it would be good work experience for his students to come and check the cottages.

It was a lot ticked off her to-do list and with Brad kindly providing paint she would at least get the bathroom, kitchen and the living-room sorted by the end of the week.

Before she went to the shops Gemma picked up her aunt's dairy again.

'I overheard Mrs Withenshaw and Edith talking about the bake off,' Gemma read. 'Neither wants me to win, but they seemed more concerned over Mrs Miller winning as she would overtake the old battle-axe on the number of wins. Why they can't just be pleased for her for winning as much as she has is beyond me. I only do it for a bit of fun and if I win then I win. If I don't, I have a nice cake to eat for afternoon tea with Mrs Compton. Let's see what they make of our Gemma's Battenberg cake, my entry for this year.'

Gemma had to smile. So that's why she'd wanted that recipe. Aunt Clara had said she wanted to make it as she was having a few friends round. Gemma had been too busy at the TV station to pay real attention to the date. It must have worked, as Aunt Clara had won first place.

There wasn't much in the diary so far; nothing seemed to be concerning her aunt, except the behaviour of one or two of the women's group — but they had concerned Aunt Clara enough for her to write it down and Gemma was starting to get a bad feeling.

'Come on, Gemma, you need to stop watching all those detective shows,' she muttered to herself.

10

Scare Tactics

Grabbing her coat and bag around midday, Gemma made her way to the front door. A loud knock stopped her in her tracks.

Opening the door cautiously, Gemma was confronted by a portly gentleman with greasy hair.

'Yes, can I help you?'

'I am Mr Bates. I believe you have received my offer for the purchase of this cottage.'

Gemma watched as the gentleman wiped his brow on a grubby handkerchief.

'Yes, my solicitor did tell me I had an offer, but I am not selling my cottage.' Her voice rose several octaves.

'Is it possible for me to come in and discuss my offer more privately?' His slimy voice grated on her nerves.

'I suppose so — you have five minutes.' Gemma stepped aside and let Mr Bates past. He was eyeing the property up and down as soon as he stepped over the threshold.

She didn't offer him a drink or ask if he would like to sit down. Instead, she tried to keep him in the hallway.

'The houses are full of subsidence, dry rot and rising damp.'

He kept a blank look on his face and Gemma felt her irritation rise. So far, apart from the leaking roof which was probably caused by a couple of loose tiles, Gemma hadn't seen any damp patches or cracks in the cottage. If these were his scare tactics, then he wasn't doing a very good job of it.

'I am not selling my aunt's house,' Gemma replied firmly.

'Oh, I believe you will eventually — you all will. By May Day this whole row of cottages will be mine and there is nothing you can do about it.'

'Why these cottages? Why not any of

the others in the village?'

Gemma was curious. There were many pretty cottages around, so why not those?

'Trucks have easy access to these, whereas further in the village the roads are too narrow.'

'Mr Bates, you cannot be seriously thinking that having a factory in the middle of the village is a good idea.' No-one would give planning permission for that, surely. At least Gemma hoped they wouldn't.

She looked at her watch.

'Your five minutes is up. Now I must ask you to leave.'

Mr Bates reluctantly walked the short distance back to the front door.

'Ms Howarth, I believe the offer I have made is more than the market value for this property.'

She looked over his shoulder to see if there was anyone there to help rid her of this parasite which had landed on her doorstep. But as usual on a weekday morning, the village square was quite dead.

The green was pristine. The trees had long since shed their leaves and new buds were just beginning to peep through.

Gemma presumed Brad was ensconced in the pub and old Mrs Compton would be no good against someone like this man.

'As I have said, I am not interested in selling — now or ever,' Gemma replied firmly. 'Oh, and according to my solicitor your offer was under market value.'

'Well, I want the cottages.'

'Mr Bates, I have had enough of you, but don't think you will be getting any of the cottages.' Gemma stood firm, one hand on the door frame. 'Now, if you will excuse me, I have things to do.'

Gemma closed the door on him and leaned back, taking huge breaths to calm her nerves. She waited behind the door until she heard his footsteps trail off into the distance.

She needed to see Mrs Compton and find out if Mr Bates had made an impromptu visit to her cottage. And she had an idea for the bake off as well, but she would need Mrs Compton's participation.

Cautiously she opened the door and peered round. Mr Bates was nowhere to be seen. Locking the door, she hurried to the end of the row and knocked.

Mrs Compton answered, still wearing a dressing gown and looking rather pale.

'Mrs Compton, are you all right?'

'Aye, lass. Just had a visit from that property developer bloke. I can't for the life of me remember his name.'

'He isn't worth remembering.'

'Come in out of the cold. I'm not feeling myself today.'

Gemma followed her inside and into the kitchen. She had a feeling that Mrs Compton spent a lot of time here, near the old range cooker.

'Gemma, you really must stop this 'Mrs Compton' stuff. I've told you my name is Daisy — no need for formalities.'

Gemma had always been told it was impolite to address her elders by their first names, but Mrs Compton kept insisting that she should do precisely that.

'Mr Bates came to see me, too,' Gemma said.

'Who's he?'

'The slippery snake who wants to buy our cottages,' Gemma replied.

Mrs Compton let out a laugh at Gemma's description.

'Oh, that's his name, is it? I could think of worse.' She stood up from the kitchen table. 'Cup of tea?'

'Daisy, sit down and I will make it for us.'

'Well, if you're sure, dear.' Sitting back down, she ordered Gemma about, telling her where everything was.

Daisy thought it was lovely to have someone young about. Since Clara died she had been on her own. The women's group were all right, but she still felt like an outcast because she wouldn't bow to the demands of Mrs Withenshaw.

'You know, I've been thinking . . . ' Daisy began absentmindedly.

'What about?' Gemma replied, taking two cups out of a cupboard.

'You were right . . . your aunt Clara didn't seem ill. Strong as an ox she was, apart from the usual colds people get.'

'I thought that, too.'

Daisy had become uneasy over the past twelve months since Clara's death. She had equalled the prize record and now she was gone, so had no opportunity to beat the old battle-axe at her own game.

'You know this bake off,' Gemma began.

'Yes, dear.'

The old lady looked at Gemma's eyes and saw the same twinkle in them that had been in Clara's.

'What if we did a joint entry? I have a great recipe for marmalade cake — using Maggie's Dundee marmalade as its main ingredient, of course.'

Daisy mulled over the proposition.

'Wouldn't that be cheating?'

'Not if we made it here and you entered it in your name only, no.' Gemma grinned. She was liking this idea more and more. 'It will teach old Mrs Withenshaw a lesson she won't forget in a hurry.'

'Let's do it. But are you sure you will have time, what with all the renovations?'

'Of course,' Gemma replied, as the kettle whistled.

Pouring two cups, Gemma sat down in companionable silence with Daisy in her lovely warm kitchen. Her plan ran through her mind. Should she decorate the cake or just leave it as it was?

'When Mr Bates came around he mentioned he was determined to get all the cottages.' Daisy's voice interrupted Gemma's thoughts and Gemma's smile was replaced by a worried frown.

11

Buried Treasure?

'Well, lass, there's been tale of a box hidden within the old school grounds,' Daisy told Gemma the next day when she called around to see her.

Gemma was all ears. The possibilities for what was in the box were endless. Did Mr Bates think there was an old hidden Saxon hoard worth a fortune, or could it have been something to do with when the school first opened?

'Is there any mention of it in books or anything?' Gemma asked.

'Only on a leaflet that the historical society produced,' Daisy told her.

'Has anyone ever found it?'

'No lass, it's just a myth. I doubt there is any box at all. But it does make for interesting debate.'

Gemma looked at her watch. She had

better get back to her own house before the men arrived to do the work.

Thanking Daisy, Gemma's head was filled with thoughts of buried treasure as well as the numerous things Mr Bates had said about the cottages.

She would soon find out if he was trying to scare her into selling her home, just as he was trying to do to the pensioners in the other cottages. As Aunt Clara used to say, not all sharks swim in the water.

Gemma made up her mind to contact the historical society and gain access to the leaflet that Daisy had mentioned, as well as read some more of Aunt Clara's diary.

'So, what are you going to get up to today, Daisy?'

'I think I'll go for a look around town and visit the bank. Nothing exciting — what about you?'

'I'm going to nip over to the shop and try this bread from Thomas's shop, then start on the painting when Brad brings the paint over later.'

'Sounds like you will be busy. Do you need anything from town?'

'No, thanks.'

Daisy put on her warm checked coat and picked up her handbag from the back of the chair.

'Why don't we have lunch together and we can discuss our cake?' Gemma offered.

'Sounds perfect, I'm looking forward to it.' Daisy smiled.

Gemma decided to head straight around to the baker's and buy some nice cakes for dessert and a few other things. Hopefully the shop would have caster sugar.

The road was quiet as usual and Gemma spotted Brad as she crossed.

'Gem!' As he waved at her from across the road, something in his voice concerned her.

'Have you seen Mrs Miller?'

'No. I haven't seen her at all since the meeting. Why? Is something wrong?'

'Well, she had asked me to fix the lock on her back door, but when I got there she wasn't there.' Brad thrust his hands into his pockets.

'Where does Mrs Miller live?'

'She lives in one of the little cottages on Chapel Street.'

Gemma was confused.

'Remind me?'

Brad laughed.

'My, you have been away too long. It's just down from the village hall and on the right.'

'Oh, I know where you mean — that's only across there.' Gemma pointed to where the village hall stood, its blue door standing out a mile in the quaint village. 'She may have just gone to the shop or to the newsagent's up on the hill by the school. I wouldn't worry, Brad.'

From the way his brows knitted together she knew he wasn't convinced.

'Gem, come over and have something to eat, will you?'

'OK, but I promised Mrs Compton I would have lunch with her so she'll be there, too.' She looked at her watch.

Eleven o'clock already.

'Sure.'

Gem dashed across the road and walked into the baker's. As she opened the door a bell tinkled and a stocky man with a moustache came out of the back room. His clothes didn't look anything special — not what she would expect a business owner to wear.

He grabbed a white apron off the hook, placing it roughly around the neck and tying it at the front.

'Hello, what can I do for you?'

'Margaret suggested I try your bread,' Gemma said.

'Sure, which one? A bloomer or a baguette?'

'A white bloomer, please.'

'I've not seen you around before.'

'No, I've just moved here. Into the old schoolhouse cottages.'

A flicker of recognition crossed his face.

'Oh, that's right. You're Mrs Howarth's niece. Been a lot of talk about you.'

'I'm sure there has been.' Gemma was already sick of the know-it-all attitude of the village and how everything seemed to stay the same. It was one reason she had needed to escape — the village was stifling her. But London was even worse, all those people in too much of a rush to bother with you.

Gemma thought of Louise, her only real friend. *You're that much of a good friend you haven't even called her since you left*, she chided herself.

She watched Thomas wrap up her bread and looked at the cakes. Lying forlornly on a cake stand were a few doughnuts which looked dry.

'Don't you have any other cakes?'

'No, not had a chance today. Been too busy getting the place ready for a health inspection,' Thomas said, handing her over the bloomer wrapped in white paper. 'I'm on my own, you know.'

'Thanks.' Gemma paid him for the loaf and went next door. She needed milk again. Perhaps a milkman would be a good thing to have.

Gemma headed out of the door, but instead of going to the mini supermarket she crossed the road to the village hall.

The cottages all seemed to be uniform, with their windows and doors all the same shade of white, except for the end one which had a brown door standing out from the rest.

Gemma hadn't asked which one was Mrs Miller's. She walked up and down the row and around the back, but there didn't seem to be any sign of life in any of them.

Giving up, she walked back towards the village supermarket. It was only small but had most things anyone could need.

She bent down to pick up a bunch of carnations from a bucket near the door. She would put those on Aunt Clara's grave later. She had some lemonade at home and thought if she put the flowers in there they may last more than a few days.

'Ms Howarth, how nice to see you again,' the woman said, but her expression was cold.

'Margaret, isn't it?'

'Yes, that's right, dear.'

A shiver ran down Gemma's spine. It was obvious Margaret didn't like her, but she wasn't sure of the reasons why.

'I'll just take these for now.' Gemma placed her basket on the counter.

'That's £8.99.'

Gemma handed over the money, took the carrier bag, muttered a thank you and left, slamming the shop door behind her. Some people just made your blood boil.

It didn't take her long to put the flowers in a vase of lemonade and the bread on the kitchen counter top.

Sinking down into the kitchen chair, she wondered why Brad was so concerned about someone who could have quite easily nipped into town and forgotten she had already made plans.

How many times had Gemma done

that herself? Made an appointment only to miss it because the show overran, or she had to remake a dish because Queenie burned whatever was in the oven.

Gemma's head was swimming with all the things she needed to do to the house. She sat racking her brain over what she could do.

12

Secret Ingredient

Checking her watch, Gemma knew it was time to fetch Mrs Compton for lunch, unless Brad had already taken her across to the Old Unicorn. She couldn't remember if she had asked him to.

Taking her purse and keys out of her handbag, she shoved them in her coat pocket and walked back outside.

The sky looked angry. Black and grey clouds danced with each other. Going out of her small wrought-iron gate she walked quickly to Daisy's at the end of the row.

Gemma smiled at the brass door knocker in the shape of a clown's head. Not that she had noticed it the night before, or even earlier when she had popped around. Daisy answered the door in the same checked coat.

'Are you ready, Daisy?'

'Lead the way, Gem.' The way Daisy had said 'Gem' reminded her of the way her Aunt Clara used to say it.

'I have a confession to make,' Gemma said, taking Daisy's arm. 'We're going to the Old Unicorn for our lunch.'

Daisy's face fell a bit.

'Oh, OK. I was so looking forward to seeing inside your cottage again.'

'How about you come back to mine after? I'm waiting for someone to come about the roof. I have cake, mince-pies and plenty of tea. I would be happy to have your company.'

This seemed to cheer Daisy up.

'That sounds wonderful.'

Arm in arm they crossed over the road and the village green to the pub. Brad would be expecting them and she wondered what delights would be on the menu today.

'Daisy, I forgot to say that Brad was meant to do an odd job for Mrs Miller, but she wasn't home. Do you know where she is?'

'Oh, my dear, don't worry about Mrs Miller, she often goes to visit a friend on Heckenhurst Avenue. She will just have forgotten.'

Gemma held the door open and let Daisy enter the pub first. It was quiet for a lunchtime, she thought.

'Have you thought about our cake?' Daisy asked her.

'Yes, I think we should make one later as a tester if you are up for it?'

'Certainly, dear, but we need to have it in by Saturday at the latest,' Daisy replied, a huge smile on her face.

'Go and find a table and I'll get us drinks. What would you like?' Gemma asked.

'I'll have a large whisky, please.'

Gemma hid her smile. Trust Daisy.

'Drinking at lunchtime?' Gemma raised an eyebrow.

Daisy wagged her finger.

'Now, listen, young whippersnapper, we will have less of your cheek.' But

Daisy laughed, too, and went to find a table. Gemma expected her to go near the fire, but instead she found a table near the French doors.

Making her way to the bar, Gemma noticed Brad had his back to her, seemingly oblivious to anyone having walked in.

'Are you going to leave us to starve then, Brad?'

He jumped.

'Gem! I wasn't sure if you were coming.'

'I said I would and I always keep my promises. Can I have a whisky and a cup of tea, please?'

'Sure, go and sit down and I'll bring the drinks across. There are menus on the table.'

Gemma walked across to Daisy.

'He's bringing the drinks over. I was wondering if we had time to decorate the cake or if it had to be plain and simple?'

'I think that if we just put maybe a small Union Jack flag or something then that should do. Whenever we have done bake offs before none of the ladies decorated them, as such. Perhaps the plates had something on them. You know your aunt Clara did a Battenberg cake once and it was just delicious, but she wouldn't give me the recipe.'

'It was my recipe she used. I'll write it down for you.'

Daisy patted her hand.

'I know you miss her. I do, too.'

Gemma hated sympathy — not because it wasn't kind, it was just that she hadn't got over her loss yet, so any mention of Aunt Clara was always hard for her to take.

'What would you like to eat?' Gemma passed over one of the menus. The shiny black case had seen better days. Even the gold lettering spelling 'Menu' was coming off. The pub seemed to be in a bit of a bad state of repair, too.

Daisy took it, nodding her thanks as they both opened their menus.

'I think I will have the steak pie, chips

and peas,' she said after a few moments.

Gemma was still contemplating the menu and finally decided on Cumberland sausage, chips and garden peas. Maybe she would have a slice of Black Forest gateau if she wasn't too full.

A waitress came over, taking their order on a neat little pad before going away again. They sat in companionable silence waiting for their food and drinks.

Gemma spoke first and pointed out that it was all very well making a marmalade cake, but there was just one problem — she didn't have a pot of Maggie's Dundee marmalade.

'Daisy, can we stop at yours and pick up a pot of the secret ingredient?'

'Of course. We will bake two when we get to yours — unless you would rather use my range?'

'I think if we use yours then no-one would be suspicious about whose cake it is.'

'That's true, but we can go and get a pot and make one at yours to eat with a cuppa.'

Brad brought the food over himself, seating himself at the table.

'Did you find out where Mrs Miller was?'

Daisy shook her head.

'As I told Gemma when she asked, Mrs Miller often goes to see a friend and all I think is that she has forgotten that you were going across.'

He shrugged his shoulders and Gemma could tell he wasn't convinced.

'Don't worry, Brad. It's nice that you are concerned, but you seem like a worrier.'

'I can't help it. It's in my make-up.' He paused. 'Do you need a hand later to paint the kitchen? It won't take long if there's two of us.'

'Sure. Come around at three if you can, or after five. I'm easy.'

'OK, I'll see you then. I'll bring that paint and brushes over.' Brad stood up and left the two ladies to finish their meal and drinks.

Gemma and Daisy didn't take long to eat. As they were finishing, the vicar opened the door to the pub. He was dressed in a dog collar and a pair of slacks, wearing old brown shoes.

He looked older now than he had when she was a child going to Sunday school. Gemma thought back to when she had taken her first Holy Communion and the prizes she had won for attending every week.

The bill came in another black folder. Gemma paid without ceremony. She had a feeling if Brad was out front he wouldn't let her pay.

'Are you ready?' she asked Daisy, pushing her own chair slightly back from the table.

Daisy had a slightly dazed look in her eyes.

'Yes, of course.'

Going back to Gemma's was a slow process. Neither of them wanted to walk too fast as they were too full after their meals.

In the archway of the church, Mrs Withenshaw stood with Margaret, who Daisy had informed Gemma was Mrs

Withenshaw's daughter, and someone else. Gemma couldn't make out who it was, and their voices were hushed so it was difficult to hear more than the odd word.

She gripped Daisy's arm tighter and hurried across towards her house as thunder clapped some distance away. It wouldn't be long before the thunder was overhead.

'I think that I may go home, Gemma, dear. I don't feel too great.'

'I can come with you if you like?'

Daisy shook her head and headed off to her cottage without so much as a backward glance.

13

Say it with Flowers

Gemma felt a little lost after Daisy had ditched her, and Brad wouldn't be coming over until later. She didn't even have any of the special marmalade, although she was sure that she had some lime marmalade in the cupboard.

The hall carpet squelched underfoot. The rain that had seeped through the roof was going to ruin the whole house unless she got it sorted out — and quick.

Gemma took out her phone, checking her bank app for the balance. The screen mocked her. She didn't have much, but it might just be enough. The longer she stayed out of work, the worse her finances were going to get.

Aunt Clara had left her a bit of money, but she didn't want to use it for anything unless it was absolutely necessary.

Gemma picked her aunt's diary up from the small coffee table and settled down to read.

'Today has been rather a strange day. Mrs Withenshaw called round. I knew what she wanted — a sneaky look at my entry for the bake off. I may be old, but I am not stupid. She is my competition, so I gave her a piece of Victoria sponge I had made for tonight's meeting. It is a good thing that I had made two. I also told her that I was going to start baking my own bread instead of going to her son's bakery. His bread doesn't taste very nice, like it used to. All the old battle-axe could say was that he had changed the flour he used. I'm sure that he is giving me inferior bread on purpose. The last loaf I had tasted salty and there was a hint of bitterness to it which I couldn't place.'

Gemma thought it was strange that she hadn't been invited to another women's meeting, but if Mrs Withenshaw had anything to do with it, the Howarth family wasn't welcome.

She walked into the kitchen, opening the cupboards, hunting around for the baking tins that she had brought. Reading her aunt's diary was making her mad, but wasn't telling her anything, either. Anger was boiling up inside her. This Mrs Withenshaw seemed like a bully. Who did she think she was?

A knock at the door interrupting her, Gemma closed the diary, placed it back on the table, and walked slowly to the door.

Standing outside the door was a rough looking gentleman in his mid-forties, his round belly hanging over his trousers. He was wearing a pair of sandy coloured paint-spattered work boots.

'I'm Stan, here to do the roof repairs.' He held out a grubby hand.

'Thanks for coming so quickly.' Gemma shook his hand.

'If it's all right with you, I will start looking at what needs to be done.'

Gemma nodded her assent.

'I will be in the kitchen if you need me. Would you like a cuppa?'

'No, not yet, thanks. I'll get on and take a break later. If this storm rolls in, you want your roof protected until I can get it finished.' His broad Lancashire twang nearly made Gemma laugh out loud as he sounded so much like Aunt Clara had done.

She also needed to get the windows done, as they were draughty and the cold breeze came into the house through all the nooks and crannies it could find.

Fixing the house and making it into a liveable state was going to be expensive if what Mr Bates was saying turned out to be true. Something made her think otherwise, though, and that for whatever reason he was out to be a scaremonger.

Picking up her phone, she called Brad over at the Old Unicorn. It was earlier than the time he had said he would come over, but she wanted to see a friendly face in an unusually unfriendly environment.

She was sure Wythorne hadn't been like this when she'd lived here before. Admittedly, that was a long time ago and as she didn't usually get involved in any of the village activities then it was entirely possible that her memory was playing tricks on her.

Putting the phone down with a satisfied smile, she started baking a practice marmalade cake. Gemma wanted Daisy to win to quieten the evil witches in the village.

Grabbing the large stone bowl out of the cupboard and the ingredients for her cake, Gemma pre-lit her oven and set about baking. The roofer would appreciate a slice, as would Brad when he finally got there.

The cake had been put in the oven by the time her doorbell rang and her heart leaped around in her chest. Brad had made her feel welcome and special in just a few short days. One thing she wouldn't do was fall head over heels for someone she had only just met.

Brad stood at the door, a bunch of red roses in his hand.

'Oh, Brad!' Gemma exclaimed. 'Are they for me?'

'Of course. I don't bring flowers if they're not for the person I'm coming to see.'

'Thank you, they are beautiful.' She leaned over and kissed his cheek. 'Come in. I'm baking and the builder's here to inspect what work needs doing and to secure the roof.'

'Smells good, whatever it is you're baking. Any for me?'

Gemma couldn't help but smile. Men always thought about their stomachs.

'Yes, there is some for you.'

Leading Brad into the kitchen, she was met by Stan.

'Excuse me, lassie, I need to go and get some plaster from the warehouse and I've seen that the roof only has a few tiles out of place. My guess is that's what's causing the leaks. I'll re-point the chimney as well.'

'No problem, Stan, do you want that drink now?'

'No, I'll try and sort these tiles out. I'm not sure exactly what else we need to do yet, but it needs to be done quickly.'

'I'll see you later, then,' Gemma said.

Part of her thought that it was an excuse for an early lunch. Wasn't that what most builders used as an excuse?

Gemma waited until he had gone before turning to Brad.

'Brad, I need to ask you something. Have you noticed anything strange happening lately?'

'What do you mean? Strange? The whole village is strange in one way or another.'

'Oh, I don't know. It's just that some people seem to be really bullish.'

Brad smiled indulgently.

'You need to lighten up. Don't forget you are a stranger around here now. It will take time to get to know people again.'

'I suppose you're right. Hey, do you want a paint party later? The icky yellow colour of this kitchen is driving me to distraction.'

'Icky? What sort of word is that? Sure, I need to head back just now, but I can come back around six or seven.'

'My word. Now shush.' She flicked him playfully with a dish towel. 'What about the pub?'

'Oh, it's quiz night,' he said, 'but normally I have a few staff working for me. I am sure they can cope without me.'

'OK. Well, I bought some flowers earlier to go on Aunt Clara's grave. It will keep me out of mischief while Stan is on the roof.'

Brad and Gemma headed out of the door together. While she had been here it seemed like she hardly spent any time indoors except for her visits to the pub and Daisy's house.

A horrid thought occurred to her.

She hadn't checked in on Mrs Long-mire since she'd said she wasn't feeling well.

She looked to her left and decided she would rectify that later.

'I'll see you later, Gem,' Brad said with a brief wave.

14

Horrific Discovery

Gemma made her way over to St John's Church. The green noticeboard had a flyer about the May Day fete and details of the daily church services.

The slabs were slippery as they always were and the huge black arched door was closed, or so it appeared from her current position. She walked past the headstones, many dotted with little spots of white lichen and moss growing on the oldest headstones. Fresh flowers were dotted around as people had remembered their loved ones, just as she was going to do.

Aunt Clara's grave was at the back of the church, turning on to the right-hand path. A sudden gust of wind whistled around the church. The stained-glass windows were just a bit too high for her to see what they were depicting.

As Gemma rounded the back of the church, she noticed a grave looked like it had been freshly dug with a piece of builder's tarpaulin covering it. Whoever was going to lie there would be right next to her aunt.

It shouldn't be so close to Aunt Clara's, Gemma thought as she wrung her hands.

Gemma tried hard to avoid standing on the sheet of tarpaulin as she walked round it to her aunt's grave. Kneeling, she began the task of clearing the dead flowers out of the vase and pushing the little stones back on to the grave. Weeds had attempted to invade Clara's final resting place.

After ten minutes the grave looked tidier, but as Gemma moved to the base of the grave to move the single weed that still remained, her foot caught on the tarpaulin and it came away.

There, underneath the tarpaulin and on top of the grass, lay the body of Mrs

Miller, dressed in a green woollen coat, a tweed skirt and a pink scarf over her head that had turned crimson.

Gemma screamed. Standing quickly, she ran around the side of the church and down the path. Grazing her hands on the archway, she ran to the pub, bursting through the doors.

'Brad! There's a dead body in the graveyard.'

He looked at her incredulously.

'Of course there are dead bodies, it's a graveyard.'

'No, there's a body.' Gemma tried gasping for breath. Why couldn't he understand? 'Mrs Miller — she's dead. In the graveyard.'

'Stay there.' He grabbed a glass and poured a brandy, handing the glass to Gemma. 'I'll be right back.'

Brad left her standing at the bar. Gemma was shaking, her mind in a whirl. Poor Mrs Miller.

Gemma couldn't think straight. Brad seemed to have been gone for ages. Her body convulsed with sobs.

Brad hurried back in.

'I've called the police. Apparently they are sending someone around straight away.'

Gemma was vaguely aware of being manoeuvred to a seat near the open fire.

'You OK?'

She nodded. It was as though the whole world was still moving and she was standing still.

'What has Mrs Miller ever done to anyone?' Gemma asked tearfully.

'I don't know, Gem, but we will find out. The police will at any rate.'

Gemma didn't know when the thought jumped into her head, but she was going to find out what happened, and also what really happened to Aunt Clara. She shouldn't have died, and neither should Mrs Miller.

After about half an hour Gemma pulled herself together.

'Brad, we need to investigate.'

He looked at her, his head tilted to one side.

'I'm not sure that is such a good idea. Have you done anything like this before?'

'No, but how hard can it be? You know everyone. Surely people talk about things when they are being served at the bar?'

'Sometimes, but not always, and most of the women who come in are cautious when they're speaking about what cake they are doing for the bake off.'

It wasn't what Gemma wanted to hear. She picked up the drinks mat, placing it on the end of the table and flipping it. When she was a child sitting in a not too similar spot as she was now, it had taken her mind off all the adult chatter.

Two uniformed police officers came into the Old Unicorn.

'Ms Howarth?'

Gemma attempted to stand up.

'Please sit down, Ms Howarth. I'm PC Morgan and this is PC Anderson. We just have a few questions for you and then Mr Houston can take you home.

'Can I please ask you what you were doing when you found the deceased?'

'She is not 'the deceased'. She is called Mrs Miller.'

'I'm sorry . . . Mrs Miller.'

Gemma looked from one to the other.

'I was putting flowers on my aunt's grave and my foot caught on the tarpaulin.' Gemma's hands flew to her mouth. She couldn't talk any more. It was so hard to talk; so hard to explain herself.

'Look, Mr Houston, I think it may be best if you take her home,' the officer said. 'We will come again later when Ms Howarth has had the chance to calm down.'

Gemma got unsteadily to her feet, allowing herself to be led back to her cottage. Stan would no doubt be wondering where she had got to and there was the cake she had left to bake in the oven.

Sighing heavily, Gemma realised it would be black by now and she only had a day to get the cake baked and delivered. Then she stopped short. How could she be thinking about baking when Mrs Miller had just died?

'Gem, are you all right?' Brad squeezed her arm.

He could feel her slipping out of his grasp. Trying to keep her upright wasn't a difficult job, but knowing what to say at a time like this was beyond him. In another hour the whole of Wythorne would know what had happened at the church.

Police cars formed a doughnut around St John's and they had put crime tape around it all.

What would happen to the May Day fete? The May Queen was due to be crowned on Sunday morning and then the fete would take place in the room downstairs and outside. If there were a lot of stalls, then a few of the stalls would occasionally work their way upstairs.

There was a man standing in the archway of the village hall, a hat pulled down covering his eyes. Brad stared at him as long as possible. There was something strange about him. Perhaps he was just waiting for someone — or was he the reason that Mrs Miller was now dead?

'Gemma, I need your house key,' Brad said to her, trying to get her to function.

'Daisy, you have to tell Daisy,' she said.

'I will go around when we have seen you back to the house,' Brad said, pushing her forward towards the little row of cottages.

He turned to look at the man who had been standing by the village hall, but he had gone. Brad frowned. Who would be standing around at that time of day apparently doing nothing?

Gemma's body still shook. Brad could feel her shiver, and as they opened the cottage door, a loud clap of thunder sounded above them.

Eventually he led Gemma into her kitchen and settled her with a coffee. As far as he was concerned, while the roofer was still up on the roof Gemma was safe.

Brad hopped over the small wall separating the cottages and knocked on Mrs Compton's door. He waited and waited. Nothing . . . just silence.

Fear struck him. She wasn't normally this long in answering the door. Daisy spent most of her time sitting in the kitchen, so it shouldn't take too long for her to answer the front door.

Brad ran out of the gate and round to the back of the house. Daisy's large back gate was fastened. The only way Brad could get into her back yard was either by climbing over the high fence or breaking the lock.

Moving back a few feet, Brad ran towards the gate and shoulder barged it. Pain shot through his arm but the gate remained firmly shut.

With nothing left for it, he climbed over the gate. The door had frosted glass, making it hard to see inside, and the kitchen window was too high for him to see into the kitchen. Squinting through the frosted glass, Brad was shocked to see Daisy lying on the floor.

He looked around the back yard to try to find something to break the glass. A black cauldron plant pot lay behind the gate. Brad hesitated. He wasn't sure if Daisy would be angry with him.

Picking it up, Brad hurled it at the door, shattering the glass. Shards flew all over the place, littering the ground and the kitchen carpet.

Daisy hadn't moved, even with the loud shattering of the glass. Bending down, Brad checked her pulse and his heart sank.

Brad picked up the phone and dialled the emergency services.

'I need an ambulance.'

15

Will Daisy Pull Through?

On the floor lay a basket of mushrooms.

'No!' Brad shouted. 'What did you eat these for? They're death cap mushrooms! Didn't you know they're poisonous?'

There were a few cooked ones on a plate with scrambled eggs. On the wooden table sat a jar of Maggie's marmalade bearing a note with a single word: 'Gemma'.

Brad put it in his pocket, assuming that nothing was wrong with it. Gemma had told him about the planned joint entry. That wouldn't happen now.

A siren sounded outside. The ambulance had arrived. Breathing a sigh of relief, Brad prayed that it wasn't too late for Daisy to get the help that she needed.

Walking quickly to the front door he turned the key, allowing the two paramedics in.

'I think she has eaten death cap mushrooms.'

The paramedics got to work, putting Daisy carefully on a stretcher and taking her to the ambulance.

'Will you be coming with us?' they asked Brad.

'No, I will be coming along after with a neighbour. Which ward will she be in?'

'Just ask at reception.'

Brad watched helplessly as Daisy was driven off in the ambulance. He needed to fix the window and take her keys with him. Locking the door after him, he went back to Gemma's house.

Gemma was sitting on the sofa exactly where he had left her.

'Did I hear an ambulance?'

'Yes, Gem, it's Daisy. She's been rushed to hospital.' He paused. 'I think she has been poisoned.'

Tears streamed down Gemma's face

as Brad took the seat next to her, bringing her into his embrace.

'How . . . ' Gemma managed to utter.

'Death cap mushrooms. It looks as though she had eaten them with some scrambled eggs. A basket on the floor was full of them. We need to call the police.'

'Daisy didn't go into Hunswood Woods. It would be too much for her, so why would she have a basket of picked mushrooms? Does anyone sell them?'

'Not that I know of, and I wouldn't make that sort of mistake.'

Gemma felt the tears pricking the back of her eyes.

'I'm going to find out who hurt Daisy. They will regret messing with my friends.'

'We will. You can't do this alone.' Brad gave her a quick squeeze, abruptly getting off the sofa. 'Do you mind if I get your roofer to fix Daisy's door?'

Gemma looked at him, her head

tilted to one side.

'Why would Daisy need her door fixing?'

'I had to smash it to get in. Before I forget, this was on the kitchen table for you,' he replied, handing her the jar of marmalade he had picked up.

'Thanks, that was for our cake. It's meant to be at the church tomorrow.' Gemma didn't think that she would bother entering the bake off. She hadn't seen Edith or Mrs Longmire since the women's meeting. Although she hadn't searched them out, what with one thing or another, it hadn't happened.

Suddenly, there was a loud knock on Gemma's door.

'Stan, have you finished?' Gemma asked.

'Aye, I have for now,' Stan said.

'Stan, could you make a door secure?'

'Yes, I can, just tell me where.'

'Brad will show you — and thanks, Stan.'

Brad left her alone. Although she had

been so glad of his company, her aunt's diary was sitting there, waiting to be read.

Gemma's blood ran cold as she read the next entry.

'I received some really nice mushrooms today. It was strange that they were brought by a delivery driver. I shall enjoy those for my tea. There's nothing better than a mushroom omelette.'

At least I now know how she died — what I don't know is why, Gemma thought. Mrs Miller and now Daisy . . . Wythorne was turning out to be anything but a nice quaint English village.

Gemma decided she would go straight to the hospital and work out what to do on the way there. The police said they would come if they had any more questions for her. Would the police investigate what happened to Daisy, or would they see it as an accident?

* * *

It took Brad half an hour to return. Gemma spent the time pacing around the living-room, trying to put the pieces together but ending up none the wiser. She put her aunt's diary back on the table.

'Gem, do you want to go and see how Daisy is?'

'Does she have any family?'

Brad looked thoughtful.

'That I don't know. She never mentioned any to me. Perhaps Mrs Longmire would know. I'd ask Mrs Withenshaw, but you have already discovered what the witch is like.'

Gemma nodded her agreement.

'Let's go to the hospital. I need to see Daisy.'

Grabbing her handbag, coat and keys, she headed off with Brad. It would take more than 15 minutes to get over to the hospital.

As they left, Gemma noticed a crowd of people standing around the entrance to St John's church rubbernecking, no doubt wondering when the police would tell them what was going on.

Did it matter about the fete if Daisy wasn't with her? Gemma was only doing a cake to help get one over on that old busybody, Mrs Withenshaw.

'Brad, I think we have a problem.'

'You don't say.' Gemma didn't miss the sarcastic tone in his voice.

'I think my aunt was murdered,' she continued. 'That same person murdered Mrs Miller, and Daisy was nearly his or her next victim.'

They sped past terraced houses as they made their way to the hospital, evening traffic making the journey take a bit longer than it would have otherwise.

They made their way past the football ground instead of going the quicker way, but she wasn't complaining. As long as they got there in time to see Daisy . . . if this was to be their last goodbye.

Unfortunately, Gemma wasn't full of confidence that she would live. After reading the diary and seeing what had happened to poor Mrs Miller, nothing was to be taken for granted.

* * *

The hospital was a mixture of old and new buildings — a bit of a rabbit warren like many hospitals. They followed the signs to the Accident and Emergency department, ambulances and cars rushing here and there. Cars filled almost every available space.

Eventually, after what seemed like hours driving around the buildings, they found a parking space near to the ENT building. It would take them as long to get back to where they wanted to be, but at least they had a space. Gemma got out of the Rolls, closing the door gently before locking it.

Gemma wrapped her arms around herself. The worry over Daisy threatened to eat her up. The only good thought zooming around her head was that Daisy was in the right place to get all the help she needed.

Gemma made up her mind to investigate Mrs Miller's murder. If nothing else it would keep her mind occupied from all her money problems.

'Daisy will be OK. Just have faith in the medical staff,' Brad said.

'I wish I had as much confidence as you,' Gemma said reluctantly.

They walked in silence through the doors of the hospital's A and E department. One receptionist with bright red hair was busy taking a call while another was seeing to someone else's query. Gemma waited, tapping her foot on the tiled floor.

Information posters were dotted along the grey walls and an electronic board gave the patients updates on wait times.

It took five minutes until the red-haired receptionist was free to speak to her.

'Can I help you?' she asked.

'My neighbour Daisy Compton has been rushed in. Can you please tell me what ward she is on?'

'I'm sorry, but I'm not sure I can tell you anything as you're not a relative.'

'I'm the only person she has. Daisy hasn't got any family.'

The receptionist excused herself and left Gemma standing there open-mouthed. She looked to Brad who just shrugged his shoulders.

Gemma avoided doctors and hospitals as much as possible — in fact, she couldn't remember the last time she'd had to go to either for herself. Just as she was bemoaning the waiting times in hospitals, the receptionist came back.

'I've just talked to my supervisor and her notes say a Ms Gemma Howarth was going to come.'

'Yes, that's me.' Gemma took her purse out of her bag and showed the receptionist her driving licence.

'If you take a seat over there, I'll get someone to come and collect you.'

Gemma and Brad made their way over to the blue waiting room chairs. Even though they had only been sitting there for a few minutes, it felt like hours, and she supposed that some of the people in A and E had been waiting that long.

Without her realising it, Brad had taken her hand in his.

Just when she was about to go back to the reception desk and ask what was happening, a doctor in green scrubs approached.

'Ms Howarth, I'm Dr Nartu. Mrs Compton is critical but stable. We have given her silibinin. Although silibinin is an experimental drug it has been shown to work.'

'You're treating Daisy like a guinea pig?'

'Gemma, the doctors are doing what they can. You need to calm down!' Brad had almost shouted at Gemma.

She shrank in her chair. Gemma hated arguments.

'I'm sorry, Dr Nartu.'

'Come with me and I'll take you to see Daisy. You have to know that she is connected to machines and it can look scary, but we're keeping her sedated for a few days. We are hoping that by keeping her in an induced coma we can minimise any damage caused by the death cap poisoning.'

'I understand,' Gemma replied and followed the doctor through the myriad corridors until they reached ICU where Daisy was in a room on her own.

Tears streamed down Gemma's face as she saw how frail Daisy looked. Brad steered her to a chair.

'Just buzz if you need anything,' the doctor said before closing the door, leaving the two of them alone.

'Brad, she looks so . . . ' The words stuck in Gemma's throat.

'I know, but the doctor seems optimistic that she will recover.'

'Who did this, and why Daisy?'

'What do you mean? No-one did this. She just picked bad mushrooms.'

'Haven't we already established the fact that Daisy wouldn't go into the woods? She certainly couldn't walk there, and as far as I know she doesn't have a car. There is no way she picked those mushrooms. Someone must have given them to her.'

'Look, Gem, I know how odd it looks, but come on, you need to be realistic. It was just an accident. There's nothing more to it,' Brad said, a touch of anger in his voice.

Why didn't he believe her? Things were strange . . . first Mr Bates and now Daisy and poor Mrs Miller? Gemma was having trouble putting the pieces together.

Suddenly a screeching alarm sounded from one of the machines hooked up to Daisy. Gemma pressed the red emergency button whilst Brad ran out of the room to get help.

Four nurses and a doctor rushed into the room.

'You need to wait outside,' the doctor said.

Gemma nodded meekly. Shakily she stood up and walked out of the room into the grey corridor. A nurse's station was opposite Daisy's room. Signs for the toilets and bathroom stuck out on the bare walls of the ICU.

Gemma thought that they might have tried to brighten the place up for the visitors at least. The doctor had been right that all the machines were scary.

A nurse came out of Daisy's room and approached them.

'She's stable now, but my advice is for you both to go home. If you let us have your contact details, we will phone if there is any change.'

Gemma wanted to cry but held it back. Her emotions were all over the place. It was hard to admit that she had grown attached to Daisy in the brief time that she had known her. Having already lost one person she cared about, she wasn't prepared to lose another.

Something had to be done.

16

Help is at Hand

Brad and Gemma left the hospital in silence. Not a word was spoken all the way back to Wythorne; both too deep in their own thoughts to talk. A velvet black sky twinkled with the stars and a full moon lit up the night sky. Gemma couldn't believe they had been at the hospital for so long.

'Brad, I've been thinking. What if the deaths of Aunt Clara and Mrs Miller are connected?'

'No, I don't think that's possible,' Brad replied, keeping his eyes on the road.

'OK.' Gemma wasn't in the mood to argue.

She made up her mind to speak to Mrs Longmire as she seemed to know Mrs Miller the best. Hopefully when the police got in contact again they might tell her something.

Brad dropped her off at the cottage.

'I have to get back to the pub. Why don't you come with me? You can help me close up.'

'Thanks, Brad, but I'm going home and having a bath. I need to relax.'

Gemma always had a bath rather than a shower if she had had a particularly dreadful day at the television station. She looked at the end cottage. Mrs Longmire's lights were on. She would go and talk to her first and give her the news about Daisy.

Gemma waited until Brad had parked his car outside the Old Unicorn and disappeared through the door. She didn't like lying to him. After all, she had promised to take it easy and relax.

Making her way along the cottages, she spotted two people by the village hall. In this light she couldn't see clearly who they were.

Strange, she thought. Why would people be at the village hall at this time?

There were no lights on in the hall so she couldn't think that anything was happening tonight. Then again, Gemma didn't know much about what went on in the village.

Mrs Longmire's lights were on downstairs, so Gemma rang the bell, waiting patiently for Mrs Longmire to answer the door. The front door had a stained-glass window at the top of the door depicting a witch flying on her broomstick by the moonlight.

Gemma had to smile — it was a typical image of the Lancashire Witches or the Pendle Witches, depending on which name you preferred. Or perhaps it was a picture of Mrs Withenshaw. Gemma chuckled at the notion.

Just then the door opened. Mrs Longmire stood there wearing a red dressing gown and red slippers.

'Gemma! What brings you out this late?'

'Mrs Longmire, I have some bad news,' Gemma said gently. 'It's Mrs Miller . . . she died earlier today.'

'Oh, poor Mrs Miller! Such a fun person to be around.'

It wasn't quite the reaction that Gemma had expected, and it must have shown on her face.

'Losing people at my age is to be expected.'

'Mrs Longmire, Mrs Miller was murdered.'

Mrs Longmire gasped and tears now poured down her face.

'Who would do such a thing?'

'I don't know — but I will find out,' Gemma said.

'Come in. It's cold outside,' Mrs Longmire said as she moved aside to allow Gemma to enter.

Mrs Longmire's house was very cluttered. Books lay on every step of the hallway stairs and even lined the hallway. Gemma supposed this was due to her being an ex English teacher. She was bound to have a love of books.

'Come through to the kitchen and I'll put the kettle on.'

'Thanks,' Gemma replied.

The kitchen was filled with as many books as the hallway and Gemma wasn't sure there was enough room for her to sit down.

'Oh, just move those books. I really do need a clear out.'

Gemma laughed but she felt guilty for doing so.

'It's hard to get rid of the books, but I know they are taking over.'

'I agree.' Gemma nodded.

'Sit down, dear.' Mrs Longmire hunted around in her cupboards for cups and saucers.

Gemma watched as she prepared the tea but didn't speak.

'You've gone all quiet,' Mrs Longmire said.

'I'm sorry. I've just been to see Daisy at the hospital.'

'Daisy is in hospital?' Mrs Longmire looked horrified.

'Brad found her earlier. She had eaten death cap mushrooms and I'm not entirely sure it was an accident. I was wondering what you could tell me about the people in the village,' Gemma replied matter-of-factly.

'I don't understand . . . '

'Well, death caps are available in Hunswood Woods, but Daisy never went there, so how did she get them?' Gemma paused. 'And she told me she always went and got her shopping herself. Obviously no-one would sell them.'

'Drink your tea, dear,' Mrs Longmire said, handing her a cup.

'Thanks.'

'Well, where can I start?' Mrs Longmire thought for a moment. 'Mrs Miller and I were close. Every Saturday night we would go to the bingo together. In fact, we did almost everything together.'

Mrs Longmire pulled at her heart strings. Gemma felt so bad that she had lost her friend.

'Is there anything I can do for you?'

'No, my dear, I am all right.'

But Gemma didn't believe her.

'Can you tell me about the baking

contest? I feel that may be the key to all this.'

Mrs Longmire nodded.

'The bake off was the vicar's wife's idea. It started as a friendly competition, but turned into a major competition between the ladies in the village.' She took a small sip of tea and then continued her tale. 'Then it started getting serious between everyone.'

'How do you mean?'

'Oh, Gemma. Friendships got ruined for a while. Then it settled down when Mrs Miller won a few times and your aunt. People took it so seriously and that's ridiculous — it's meant to be a fun day celebrating May Day and the May Queen.'

'Did Mrs Miller have any enemies?'

'No, everyone liked her. She never said a bad word about anyone. Don't get me wrong, she may have thought things, but if she did, it never came out of her mouth.'

'I wish I had known her,' Gemma replied sincerely. 'What about everyone else? Did they feel the same way about the bake off?'

'Oh, yes. A lady called Rita had declared last year's bake off winner to have cheated.'

Gemma leaned forward, her head in her hands and her elbows on the table. She was curious how people turned nasty whenever there was a competition. It didn't matter who or what the competition was, it always ended up with someone being a sore loser.

'Mrs Longmire, have you had a letter asking to buy the cottage?'

'Call me Elizabeth, and yes, I have had several nasty letters. They all say the same thing — that there is something wrong with the cottages and they need to be condemned, that sort of thing.'

'I phoned the local college,' Gemma told her, 'and asked if they could send some students to survey the cottages and see if there is subsidence.'

'That would put my mind at ease,' Mrs Longmire said with a hopeful tone in her voice. 'Are you entering the bake off, dear?'

'No, I wasn't going to. I think being a newcomer and everything, it would look bad if I got any sort of rosette. I can see a few feathers being ruffled. Daisy was going to enter, I think.'

Gemma realised what she had just said. There was no entry — they hadn't baked anything, and did she want to after today?

'I'd better go, I've kept you long enough,' Gemma said as she rose from the kitchen chair. It was getting late and if Daisy was going to enter the contest she would need to get baking, especially as she had only done one test cake earlier in the week.

'Don't be a stranger,' Mrs Longmire said as she got up and walked Gemma to the door.

After bidding each other goodnight, Gemma walked back to her cottage debating on whether she would bake a round or a square cake.

A load of building materials had

appeared on her path, no doubt from Stan who had said he was going to order some. She must have missed the part where he said he was leaving it all out for her to trip over.

Tutting to herself, she unlocked the front door to find a flyer of some sort on her mat. Picking it up, she unfurled the piece of paper.

'With the May Day celebrations on Sunday, we at the village council find that all your building supplies and ostentatious car are extremely unsightly and need to be moved by tomorrow. Your car will be towed if this is not complied with.'

Gemma's blood boiled. Who did they think they were? There were far more conspicuous cars coming in and out of the village. As for the building materi-als, they hadn't been here when she had gone to the hospital. Someone on the village council was being nasty for the sake of it.

Wandering into the kitchen and switching on the light, Gemma started taking ingredients out of the cupboards and placing them all on the table.

She took out three different shaped cake tins, and would decide which one to use after the mixture was done. The old brown stone bowl of her aunt's was just perfect for making a large amount of mixture in. She had doubled the ingredients so that she could make two in case she made a mistake. Well, all the best cooks did make mistakes — no-one was perfect. She chuckled as she remembered all the mistakes she had made whilst cooking for the show.

After 15 minutes she had a nice mixture, putting half in a heart-shaped tin and the other in a square tin. Leaving it to bake, she made herself a coffee and a sandwich, taking both into the front room.

She looked closely at the trophies that stood on the mantelpiece. Gemma had moved them when she was cleaning up and making everything in the house liveable. She was sure that the bake off held the key to things. The problem was, she wasn't sure how or why.

Picking up her aunt's diary, she read another entry.

'I'm tired of living here in Wythorne alone. I wonder if Gem has room for her old aunt. Gemma was always such a bright young thing. I'm just sick and tired of all the backstabbing that goes on. People you think are friends cannot wait to tittle-tattle behind your back. I don't think I have any real friends here except for Daisy. She is really honest and genuine.'

It made Gemma feel worse. If only her aunt had asked her, she could still be alive now. Working for the TV station, she'd had enough money for both of them.

Hot tears fell on to her cheeks as the guilt she now felt threatened to eat her up. She placed the diary on the small table and went to check on the cakes. Gemma found it hard to see with her eyes still filled with tears.

She took the cakes out and left them

on the cooling rack just as her front door bell rang.

'Who's calling at this time?' she said loudly.

She answered the door to find Brad standing there, clutching a bottle of wine and a plate covered with a silver lid.

'I didn't think you would have eaten yet.'

'No, I haven't. Do you want to come in? I could use the company.' Gemma automatically opened the door wider and moved aside to let him in.

'Why have you been crying?'

His voice was sincere and full of warmth.

'I've been reading Auntie Clara's diary. She wanted to leave here and live with me. I should have asked, I should have thought about her — not just myself.'

Brad put the things down on the hall table and pulled Gemma into a hug as she cried into his shoulder. He felt bad that she had lost her only family, but if he knew anything about Clara it was that she was too proud to ask her niece. Gemma just needed to realise that it wasn't her fault.

He stroked her back tenderly. For the first time in his life he had someone to care about. Brad knew from the moment he'd first seen Gemma step out of her car that she was the one for him, but now wasn't the time to tell her how he felt.

'Come on, let's get you sitting down and having some food before you end up fainting.' He let go of Gemma and picked up the plate and the bottle of wine, which now seemed like a bad idea.

Gemma just shrugged, her eyes red and puffy from all that crying. Her hair, once glossy and silky, now looked dull and lifeless.

'You look like a red-eyed panda,' Brad said with laughter in his voice, trying to lighten the mood.

'Am I meant to take that as a compliment?'

'Sorry, I couldn't resist,' Brad replied. 'Now eat your food before it gets cold.'

He made Gemma sit at the table whilst he rooted around in her cupboards and drawers for glasses and cutlery. She still looked sad and he wasn't sure that anything he said would cheer her up.

'Gem, what's really the matter?'

'It's about everything that has happened. What was Mrs Miller doing in the graveyard? The police haven't been in touch to let me know what's happening. They haven't left a phone message while we were at the hospital.'

'OK, let's go through this logically. Mrs Miller could have been killed last night or today, which is unlikely because someone would have seen whoever it was in broad daylight.'

'I remember at the women's meeting they said there would be another meeting on Wednesday to finalise the May Queen and attendants' outfits. I wasn't invited to that,' Gemma said thoughtfully.

'So, on that assumption she would have been at the church last night. Now I need you to think hard. How did she look? Could you see any wounds?'

'I could see blood, but as soon as I found her, I ran to you for help,' Gemma said. 'I don't know how she was killed or why, or who killed her — but I am going to find out,' she added determinedly.

'I will help, but you need to be careful, Gem. Whoever it was is dangerous.'

'Stating the obvious, Brad?' Gemma laughed weakly, but she knew that he was only being friendly.

'Look, Gem, I think once you have finished your food you need to go to bed.'

'Brad, would you stay?' Brad looked quizzically at her. 'I have a spare duvet and pillow,' she added quickly.

'I'll sleep down here on the sofa?' Brad asked.

'There is always the spare room. I can get it cleaned and ready for you?'

Gemma offered.

'No, it's OK. We will start on the painting tomorrow or get Stan to start.'

Half an hour later Gemma brought Brad the spare bedclothes so he could make a makeshift bed up on the sofa. She didn't want to be alone tonight. With one person dead and another in hospital, the whole business had really shaken her up.

17

So Many Questions . . .

Light shone through the curtains. Throwing off her duvet and getting out of bed, Gemma had a quick wash and got dressed before going down into the kitchen to make a morning cup of tea.

Brad lay coiled like a cat on the sofa, snoring softly. Closing the door gently behind her, Gemma walked into the kitchen.

Grabbing a notepad and a pen out of the drawer, she began to make a list of people she wanted to talk to, then wrote down what had happened the day before.

Gemma decided to use the electric kettle. It didn't make as much noise as the stove one and she didn't want to wake Brad.

The kitchen looked different. Empty

paint tins lay by the back door and a tin sitting on the counter by the door contained paint brushes.

The kitchen had that awful new paint smell. How had she not noticed it when she first came downstairs?

Gemma smiled. Brad must have decorated the entire kitchen whilst she slept. It was no wonder he was still asleep. She hadn't fully woken herself as she hadn't yet had her customary three cups of tea before she was ready to face the world.

She would have to repay Brad for painting her kitchen whilst she was asleep.

After her third cup of tea, Gemma decided she would wander over to the shop. It was a great place for village gossip — or at least it used to be.

Quietly closing the door behind her, she crossed the village square and headed towards the shop. The baker's was open as normal and she almost bumped into Mr Bates as he came out from the baker's with a loaf tucked under his arm.

He approached her with a sly smile on his lips.

'Ms Howarth, how very nice to see you.'

'I have nothing to say to you,' Gemma retorted.

'I can't believe I have been so lucky to get the opportunity to buy two of the cottages. Just the other three to purchase and I will have them all.'

'Really? And which two would they be?'

'Mrs Miller's and Mrs Compton's.'

'As Mrs Miller didn't live in the old school house, you will have a job with that one. As for Mrs Compton — she is alive and well and not planning on going anywhere any time soon.'

With that, Gemma pushed past him, her insides churning. Who did he think he was?

The shop door tinkled as she opened it. Margaret was putting new stock on the shelves.

'Hi, Margaret,' Gemma said more cheerfully than she felt.

'Gemma, how nice to see you. Have you heard about poor Mrs Miller?'

'Yes, I found the body,' Gemma said as she grabbed a basket.

'Oh, you poor thing. That must have been a terrible shock for you.'

Margaret didn't sound at all sincere.

'Yes, it was a shock, then poor Mrs Compton was taken ill and is now in hospital.' Gemma wasn't sure if she should have said that.

'Oh, that means she won't be entering the annual bake off. What a shame.'

'No, she already had her entry done. Brad is taking it across for her.'

The look of horror on Margaret's face was a picture.

'It's just a friendly competition after all,' Gemma said.

'There's some round here that think it's the be all and end all to everything. Take your aunt Clara; she was one of those that had to win.'

Gemma wanted to retort that her aunt had thought of it as fun and had hated the way the contest had turned out to be taken so seriously.

'Did she?' Gemma said. 'Auntie Clara never really mentioned the bake off. She did always talk about the May Queen and her attendants, though.'

'Really? I'm surprised. Mum always takes it seriously and hates to lose. Like last night at the women's meeting, which, by the way, I noticed you were absent from . . . '

'I would have been there if I had been invited,' Gemma snapped back.

'Mrs Miller was explaining as we walked out of the church how she was going to win. Took a recipe off a TV show, or so she said,' Margaret said.

'Well, that isn't against the rules, is it?'

'No, but still. Can't say that I'm sad she's gone. We didn't really see eye to eye.'

'I see that slimy Mr Bates is still hanging around the village.' Gemma changed the subject.

'Oh, he isn't that bad. As far as I am

concerned he is just doing his job like me or Thomas.'

Really, Gemma thought. What about writing nasty letters, wanting all the houses in the converted school house? Yes, it was prime residential property and a main feature in the village square, but they were people's homes and would not become a factory.

'Can I get you anything, Gemma?' Margaret asked.

'Er, no, I've forgotten what I needed. I'll pop back later.'

Gemma left the shop and returned home. As she opened the door she heard the kettle whistling.

'Brad?'

'In the kitchen, Gem!' he hollered.

'Brad, I've just had an interesting conversation with Margaret over at the shop.' She smiled at Brad's dishevelled look, his bed hair and creased clothes.

'I need to thank you for painting the kitchen,' she added. 'You can't have had much sleep.'

'Oh, a couple of hours. I'll make up

for it tonight. It's my day off tomorrow so I'll get a decent lie-in. The bar staff know not to disturb me unless it's an emergency.'

Gemma giggled.

'Anyone would think you have an easy life as a landlord.'

'Delegation — that's the key, Gem.' Taking cups from the draining board, Brad held one up. 'Tea?'

'Yes, please.'

As Brad got on with making the tea, Gemma suddenly had a thought. She needed to phone the hospital.

She went back into the hallway, grabbed the telephone handset and dialled the number for ICU.

'Hello, I'm Gemma Howarth. I'm just enquiring as to how Daisy Compton is . . . Oh, that's great. I will come and see her later. What time are visiting hours?'

She put the phone down with a smile. Daisy would be OK.

Brad stood expectantly.

'Well?'

'Daisy is going to be all right.'

Brad rushed and hugged Gemma, placing a kiss on the top of her head.

'That's really great, Gem. Shouldn't I drop Daisy's entry off?' As he said it, Gemma saw him look at the cake tin on the side.

'Yes, I think you should.' Gemma nodded in agreement. 'Brad, do you think you can speak to Mrs Withenshaw and see how she feels about Mrs Miller's death?'

'Yes, but why would you want me to talk to her?'

'I'm not sure, I just have a bad feeling.'

Gemma played with her hands as she always did when she was nervous. Whilst Brad was going to do that, she was going to go to Townley Hall and pick up the leaflet on the supposed treasure of the old school house. Not that she would find anything significant, or at least she hoped she wouldn't.

'Where did you go and why didn't you wake me?' Brad demanded.

'You looked so peaceful that I didn't think it was right after you had painted the kitchen whilst I slept,' Gemma replied. 'I went to see Margaret over at the shop. She didn't seem bothered about Mrs Miller. I didn't tell her why Daisy was in hospital, though. I had thought of going to see Thomas, but I haven't had a chance yet.'

'I'll go over to see him,' Brad offered. 'I could do with some fresh bread.'

'Why don't we meet back at the pub for lunch and we can trade information?' Gemma suggested. 'As long as we're not overheard.'

'The old smoking room will do. Not many people go in during the week. It's only used on Sundays when the men play dominos and darts.'

'OK, it's a deal.'

Stan hadn't come over yet and he was meant to fix the boiler today, so that Gemma would have heating and more than lukewarm water. But he didn't have a key to get in.

Sitting down, Gemma put her head

in her hands and tried to think where to hide a key. If she and Brad weren't going to be in until later, then Stan wouldn't be able to get in to do any work.

'Brad, do you have your mobile handy? I need to tell Stan I'll leave a key under the plant pot at the front of the house.'

'Sure. Give me his number and I'll text him.'

Gemma got up and went back into the hall for her phone book, flicking through the pages until she found Stan's number. Brad sent him a text message then placed his cup in the sink and grabbed his jacket from the back of the chair.

'Don't forget the cake,' Gemma said with more force than she had meant.

Standing up, she rushed to get the cake tin and make sure the lid was sealed.

'Take this across to the church first, please.'

I would like to be a fly on the wall

when Brad walks in with the cake, Gemma thought.

They said goodbye to each other and Gemma placed her spare key where she had told Stan it would be. Then, jumping in the Rolls, she made her way to Townley Hall.

It wasn't far away, and as she drove up the road towards the hall she noticed some of the trees that lined the path already had tiny leaves on the branches.

The car park at the top of the road was unusually empty, as many people came up here to walk their dogs.

The large war memorial stood tall and proud as it always had. She remembered playing hide and seek around it when she was a child.

Gemma parked the car and got out. Walking through the gates on her right was the Old Stables Café, famous in its own right for appearing in the movie 'Whistle Down the Wind'. On her left was a large man-made pond filled with ducks and various plants and amphibians.

There in front of her was Townley Hall, a gorgeous mansion. For six centuries it belonged to the Townley family until it was given to the Burnley Corporation. Now this was a treasure — unlike the made-up stuff that Mr Bates was going on about.

Gemma didn't have time today to go in and look at the collections; she just needed the leaflet from the little gift shop.

Opening the large glass door, Gemma scanned the shop to see if she could spot where the leaflets were kept. Not seeing anything, she approached the counter.

'Excuse me, do you have a leaflet on the old school house in Wythorne, please.'

'I'm not sure we have any left. Someone came in last week and took the last one.' The woman behind the counter went over to a rather distinguished-looking gentleman, engaging him in conversation. After a few minutes she came back.

'I'm sorry. We don't have any more of the leaflets at the moment.'

'You don't know who took the last one, do you?'

What sort of question is that, Gemma chided herself. With so many visitors, how could she expect the woman to know that.

'No. I'm sorry, I don't.' The woman shook her head.

Gemma thanked her and walked back down the path to the car park. She would have plenty of time to come back and have a decent look round. Although she was no stranger to the beautiful grounds of Townley, it was a lovely place to come.

Once in the car she wanted to phone Brad, but she didn't have a mobile. Her old one had belonged to the TV company. She had had to return it and hadn't got round to replacing it with one of her own.

Gemma reasoned that the murder had nothing to do with the cottages because Mrs Miller didn't live there

— she lived around the corner.
Daisy, on the other hand, did live in the cottages, but were the two acts linked or had someone just made a mistake?

18

A Strange Affair

Gemma drove home without really thinking about where she was going. Her autopilot had kicked in. If she was being realistic she didn't have a clue where to start.

Being an armchair detective whilst watching a TV programme was all very well, but not when it was real life.

She planned on seeing Daisy again this afternoon, but right now it seemed all she was doing was running around and getting nowhere. Perhaps if she sat and wrote things down it would help clarify her ideas.

Brad would be in the pub working. Saturday was his day off, so she planned on inviting him over for dinner. Perhaps he could be convinced to pick her up a mobile phone.

She found herself going down New Street. The small off-licence was still there. She hadn't noticed it even though she had driven up and down the road a few times. Too much on her mind, that was the problem.

Her old junior school was on her left with its playing field. The school felt so open it was a joy to go to school. The newsagent's was just across the road.

She smiled at the memory of going in to get an extra comic and some sweets before going home. Her aunt used to have 'Twinkle' delivered for her.

Pulling into her parking space in front of the cottage, she saw that Edith, Mrs Withenshaw and Thomas were standing talking by Edith's gate. Cautiously she got out of the car.

'Morning!' she called.

'Morning, Gemma. I've just heard about Daisy,' Thomas said.

This was perfect — she would maybe get some information.

'Yes, she is going to pull through.' As

Gemma watched them, a dark cloud passed over Thomas's face, then, just as suddenly as it had appeared, it had gone.

Edith was wearing black trousers and matching jacket, a purple scarf around her neck. Mrs Withenshaw had a mismatched ensemble. Thomas was still wearing his black and white trousers and white apron.

'I hear she picked some bad mushrooms,' Mrs Withenshaw said.

'That is how it appears. I doubt she went out and picked them herself, though,' Gemma snapped.

'Mrs Miller should have been more careful on the stone flags. How silly of her letting something scare her.'

Gemma was fuming. Didn't she have any heart?

'Well, accidents happen, don't they? I need to make a call, so I will see you both later.'

Turning her back on the small group, she walked into her house. She was greeted with banging and clanking.

'Stan?' She shouted his name over the noise, but he obviously hadn't heard her.

She walked into the kitchen to find Stan standing half in and half out of the larder. She tapped him on the shoulder to get his attention.

'Do you want a brew, Stan?'

'Aye, lassie, I wouldn't say no. Boilers almost done. I've just got to tighten this pipe up and turn the gas on,' Stan replied without looking at her.

In the meantime, Gemma went through to the living-room and took out her aunt's diary, hoping she might find some words of comfort. Opening it at a random page, the words she read made her gasp.

'Stan Dowling popped around earlier. He asked about our Gemma. I wish he would contact her himself. It's just a shame that her mother and he never got married before she died. Gemma looks so like her father it is uncanny. One day, perhaps, they will meet.'

Stan? The same Stan who was sitting

in her kitchen at this very moment? Gemma had no idea how to broach the subject with Stan. Perhaps the best course of action was to wait until the right opportunity arose.

Gemma made them both tea, placing the cups on the kitchen table and hoping Stan didn't notice how her hands were trembling.

Grabbing a notepad and pen out of the drawer, she went through to the living-room and started to make notes on the possible murder and Daisy's poisoning.

She couldn't remember telling anyone about how Daisy was poisoned. Did Brad tell anyone?

Mrs Withenshaw's comments about Mrs Miller were also strange. No-one would know what had really happened until there was an inquest or more questions had been asked by the police.

Gemma made her mind up to ring the police and ask to speak to PC Anderson to find out if he had any new information. There was something strange about the whole affair.

'There, your new boiler's in. Should have a nice warm house soon,' Stan said as he turned around, a spanner still in his hand.

'Thanks, Stan, I appreciate your hard work,' Gemma replied.

'Stan, have you heard any rumours about treasure here in the old school house?' she added.

'Aye, I did hear something a long time ago. The old school made a time capsule and for a long time the kids called it their treasure. My great-grandma told my mum about it, as she went to school here. Then when they built the new school they closed this one and turned it into the cottages. They're listed buildings, you know.'

Gemma laughed a hard belly laugh. Mr Bates would be highly disappointed — the cottages were listed so they couldn't be knocked down for a factory!

So what did he really want? She needed to have a word with the slimy

Mr Bates and see what his game was.

The kitchen was starting to warm up already. Perhaps tomorrow morning she wouldn't wake up freezing for once.

'Is there anything else you need me to do?' Stan asked as he drank the last dregs of tea.'

'No, not at the moment. I want to thank you for doing the work. It's just the roof now.'

'Well, if it's OK with you I'll come back tomorrow to finish the roof off.'

'Sure, Stan, that would be great.'

Gemma gave him a warm smile. He had done wonders in the few days he had been working on the house. She had to force him to take a break, but she had told him to make himself tea whenever he wanted. It was only fair with her running here, there and everywhere.

Gemma was just about to make them another brew when the doorbell rang.

19

Under Suspicion

Gemma went to the door, opening it slowly. Standing on her doorstep was PC Anderson.

'Officer, can I help you?'

'Yes, you can. I need some more information about what you saw yesterday. We can do it here or down at the station — the choice is yours.' His voice was very authoritarian.

'Come in,' Gemma said, keeping her voice even.

She led the officer into the kitchen where Stan was. She felt it was far safer to have a witness when she was being questioned.

PC Anderson took his police notebook out of his top pocket.

'Can you tell me what you were doing in the graveyard yesterday?'

Gemma sighed.

'I've already told you all this.'

'Yes, but I want you to go over it again.'

'I got some flowers from the village shop yesterday. I went to the church to lay flowers on my aunt's grave. It needed tidying and my foot caught on a piece of tarpaulin. That's when I saw . . . ' She tried to get the words out, but they were stuck in her throat.

'Did you see anyone else?' PC Anderson asked gruffly.

'No. There was no-one around. I saw a few cars driving out of the village, but I ran straight to the pub and told Brad what I had found.'

'We've had a phone call that suggests you killed Mrs Miller.'

Gemma opened her mouth to say something, but nothing came out. She couldn't believe that someone had the audacity to say she had killed someone! What reason would she have to kill Mrs Miller? She had only met her six days ago.

'Why would I kill anyone?'

'I don't know. You tell me.' PC Anderson reached down to his belt and unhooked the handcuffs. 'So, tell me why didn't you call the police straightaway?'

'I don't own a mobile. I haven't since I left my job at the television show,' Gemma said determinedly. 'Do you know yet how she was murdered?'

'Yes, she was struck on the back of the head with a blunt object. She died where she fell, and as you know was covered up to hide her body. We think that she was going to be moved when it got dark.'

'So, am I a suspect in a murder case?'

'I'm not suggesting you are, but I would advise you to stay in the village for the time being until we have completed our investigations.'

The officer walked around the kitchen. He had put his notebook away but was twirling the handcuffs around.

Stan was still sitting at the kitchen

table and he looked as shocked as Gemma was.

'Ms Howarth, if it's OK, I'm going to get off. I'll see you tomorrow. Do you mind if I keep the spare key until then?'

'Not at all, Stan. See you tomorrow.'

Stan gathered up his tools and left the house without another word, but the police officer was still there.

'Listen,' Gemma snapped. 'I don't know what you think, but I didn't kill anyone. But you can rest assured I will find out who did.'

'Look, I don't like it any more than you do,' PC Anderson replied, 'but I'm just doing my job.'

How long would the policeman stay here insinuating things, Gemma wondered.

'What about Mrs Compton?' she asked. 'Someone tried to poison her.'

'That seems like an accident. She just went out and picked some mushrooms and she didn't check what they were.'

'No. She doesn't go out into Hunswood. It's too far for her to go by herself,' Gemma retorted.

She was getting angry at the officer because he wasn't listening to sense. Did he want an easy open and shut case? She had a feeling this was anything but.

'Ms Howarth, I would appreciate you concentrating on whatever it is you do and leave the police work to the professionals.'

With that one last dig he turned around and walked out of the house without even waiting for her to see him to the door.

All she had gleaned from his visit was that Daisy's accident was just that, and Mrs Miller had been murdered and he thought she had done it!

Well, Gemma decided, she wasn't going to take that! Of all the things she might be, a murderer wasn't one of them.

She would try to find out where Mr Bates was staying, but first she would go and see Brad.

Gemma grabbed her coat and bag

and left the house. She would need a holiday after all this running around.

The sky was pale blue, dotted with cotton-wool clouds, the air clean and fresh. Brad's car was still parked where she'd left it, but instead of going straight over to the Old Unicorn she looked left to the church, deciding to have a look around there instead.

As she approached the archway she could see that the church door was open.

Gemma smiled to herself. First she would go in and see what was going on, and if her and Daisy's cake was there for judging.

Jogging up to the door and pushing the inner glass door open, she could hear voices from upstairs. She couldn't tell who they were as it sounded like there were several people upstairs in the tower.

Gemma held on to the rail as she walked up the steps as she knew they could be slippery. You could easily fall and do some real damage to yourself.

The door to the room in front of her was wide open, so she walked in and leaned against the door frame and watched.

'Edith, the cakes go over here!' Mrs Longmire shouted.

'I know, I know. Stop being pushy, Elizabeth. I need to clean the tables first. Whoever did it last has never cleaned a table before, by the looks of all these.' Edith tutted, and Gemma wanted to laugh.

'I think Margaret cleaned them,' Edith replied.

'She wouldn't know how to clean a spoon, let alone a window.'

The two of them cackled but carried on cleaning the tables and laying out the entries, totally oblivious to her presence.

'You know, Elizabeth, it's a shame that Mrs Miller is dead. She was such a dear, sweet thing. A bit scatter-brained, but nevertheless . . . '

'Yes, I agree — and it's strange without Clara here this year. Her death was so sudden I'm not sure if it was a natural death, but who am I to say what happened?'

Just at that moment Mrs Longmire looked up, saw Gemma standing there and smiled.

'Gemma, could you give us a hand, please? Edith and I have been left all alone.'

'Of course, Mrs Longmire. Just tell me what you need me to do.'

'Could you finish wiping the tables? Then Edith and I can finish putting the tablecloths on them.'

'Yes, certainly.'

'Oh, and Gemma, you can call me Elizabeth,' she said with a smile.

'Gemma,' Elizabeth continued, 'I was wondering how you think your aunt died. I'm sorry you overheard our conversation, but what with Mrs Miller and all . . . '

'I don't know. I've found her diary and learned she was thinking of moving down to London with me. I wish she had told me.'

Edith patted her hand.

'I'm sorry, love.'

Edith and Elizabeth seemed sincerely sorry for her. Perhaps they were thinking of their own mortality.

'Can I ask you both something?' Gemma asked.

'Of course you may.'

'Did either of you see anything the night before last when you left the church after the women's meeting?'

Elizabeth shook her head.

'No. I left with Edith as I always do. I think that Thomas came to walk Margaret and Rose home.'

'Rose?' Gemma asked enquiringly.

'Mrs Withenshaw.'

'Oh, right. Sorry, I didn't know her first name.'

'They seemed to hang back,' Edith added. 'I saw Elizabeth back to her cottage and then I went to mine. I had a cup of tea and watched the news, then went to bed after I checked everything was locked.'

'I went straight to bed,' Elizabeth said.

'The first I heard of Mrs Miller's death was when you came and told me. If I'm honest I've not been feeling well these last few days. Don't worry, I won't bore you with the details. I think it was a bad loaf. I don't eat much except sandwiches.'

Gemma scrubbed the table harder.

Elizabeth wasn't feeling well, and Daisy was already in the hospital.

'Elizabeth, can you go to the hospital and get checked out?'

'I . . . I don't really like hospitals.'

'I hope I'm wrong, but I don't think I am. You're being slowly poisoned, and I have a feeling I know who is responsible. I just can't prove it yet.'

'You're quite the little detective, aren't you?' Elizabeth winked at her.

Gemma went over to the back wall and cleaned the last table. Edith and Elizabeth had made short work of the tablecloths and rearranging the baking entries.

'Have you had any more letters asking to buy the properties?' she asked.

'No, I haven't, thank goodness,' Edith replied.

Gemma turned to Elizabeth again.

'Look, if I get Brad to drive you, would you go to the hospital?'

'But why?'

'Just trust me, please,' Gemma implored her.

Elizabeth looked at her and then she simply nodded.

'If you don't need me any more, I'll go over to the pub and get Brad. He will wait in the car for you. Promise me you will come?'

Elizabeth brought Gemma into her embrace.

'Be careful,' she whispered in her ear.

Gemma tried her best to reassure her.

'Yes, I will be.'

Gemma left the two women alone in the room and ran down the stairs without looking to see who was in the kitchen or adjoining room. Behind her a figure moved back into the shadows and watched her leaving.

By the time Gemma arrived at the pub she was panting for breath. Brad was over by the far wall collecting glasses and wiping the tables.

'Brad, I need you to take Mrs Longmire to the hospital.'

'Nice to see you, too, Gem,' he said, kissing her cheek.

Heat rose up on the back of her neck and on to her face.

'Please, Brad, it's urgent. I think she is being poisoned, too.' Gemma stared into his eyes, imploring him to believe her.

'OK. I give in.'

She hugged him hard.

'Thank you. I said you would be waiting in the car. If you want, I can keep an eye on the pub?'

'Have you ever poured a pint?' Brad smiled wryly.

'Erm, no. How hard can it be?'

'No comment,' Brad replied as he pulled away from her embrace.

Gemma felt bereft. She was feeling things for Brad she hadn't felt in a long time. Was it possible to feel like this after such a short acquaintance?

Gemma wished she had Aunt Clara to talk to — she would have known what to do.

No, Gemma, she told herself, you need to figure this mystery out before you sort out your feelings.

'I'll give you a ring on the pub phone when we find anything out,' Brad told Gemma, 'and while I'm there I will go and see Daisy.'

Brad said his goodbyes and left Gemma in the pub. She assumed that the chef was in the kitchen making food for dinner — and unless the bar staff had turned into tables and chairs, she was alone. Brad's private quarters were up the stairs which had a locked wooden gate at the bottom.

Gemma went behind the bar and grabbed a few glasses as she tried to pour a decent pint without a ton of foam on the top.

A cold breeze rushed into the pub. Gemma turned around quickly. Walking into the pub, wearing a black leather suit and hat, was Mr Bates.

How fortuitous, she thought.

'Ms Howarth, you have a job in the local pub?'

'I'm helping out. What can I get you?' she asked shortly.

'Double whisky neat, if you know how to do that?'

'Listen, Mr Bates, if you want a drink I'd be a bit more polite if I were you,' Gemma said.

How dare he belittle her, she thought.

'That's eight pounds.'

'That's extortion.'

'If you don't want it, you can pay town prices. Oh, and while I think about it, I want to know why you are trying to buy the cottages? Don't give me any flannel about treasure that is just a child's time capsule, or a factory. You can't knock down a listed building.'

'I was hired to buy the cottages. If I managed to buy them all I was to be given a bigger fee than the amount I had already been paid. I thought Mrs Howarth's would go to auction, as I was told that was the first one to go up for sale. You ruined that by moving in and deciding to stay,' Mr Bates replied.

'You were told my aunt's was the first up for sale?'

'That's what I said, didn't I? I was told last April that the person had it on good authority that your aunt's cottage was going up for sale. Then, in May, your aunt died, and the cottage stayed empty for nearly a year until you moved in. Obviously the threatening letters that I sent to all the owners didn't work.'

'Can you tell me who hired you?'

'No. That is confidential. I am only here to get the money owed to me, then I am out of this dump.'

'There's nothing wrong with our village.' Gemma grabbed the cloth from under the bar top and began scrubbing angrily.

'You and your neighbours don't have to worry any more. Although if the old ones die then I will be buying those.'

Gemma threw her cloth down.

'They're not old!' she shouted at him.

'Whatever you say. By the end of today I will be gone — at least for the time being.' Mr Bates drank his whisky in one go, slammed the glass on to the bar and walked out.

So, you were paid, were you, Mr Bates, Gemma mused.

Whoever wanted the cottages was happy to kill for them. It was the only logical explanation — or was it?

The death of two people and the poisoning of two others — were the cottages the reason for all this?

Brad wouldn't be back for a few hours and she could only wait and ponder.

Gemma didn't like being alone at the moment, too many things could go wrong.

While the pub was empty she went around all the tables, wiping them clean, even though Brad had already done it. It gave her something to do.

Then the telephone behind the bar began to ring.

20

Dangerous Territory

The phone continued its incessant tone. Gemma walked over and picked up the handset.

'Hello. The Old Unicorn.'

'Gem, it's Brad. Are you sitting down?'

Gemma's heart skipped a beat and she felt sick. Being told to sit down was never a good thing.

'Brad, what's wrong?' she asked cautiously.

'Mrs Longmire has been poisoned, too. They're not sure what she has been given until they run tests. The only thing that the doctor knows for sure is that it was a different poison from the one Mrs Compton had taken.'

'Oh my goodness, Brad. What is going on?'

'I don't know, love, but we will get to the bottom of it. I have to go, I'll see you in half an hour.'

'Brad, any chance you have the baker's phone number?'

'I think so somewhere. I'll check when I come home. Why?'

'I need to put a few more pieces together and will tell you everything when I see you,' Gemma replied.

The phone went dead, so Gemma placed it back in the cradle. With Brad gone she couldn't go back to the house to see if the diary told her any more, but she was certain now who had murdered Mrs Miller, and she believed her aunt was killed for the same reasons.

The pub was so quiet for a Friday, she realised. Had everyone been chased away?

Gemma heard a door slam from behind her and then loud footsteps.

'Brad, we have to get some better bread than this,' a male voice shouted.

'Brad's not here.'

The chef appeared wearing black and white chequered trousers and a chef's hat. Gemma thought he was a little overdressed for a pub kitchen, but who was she to reason why?

'Who are you?' he asked abruptly.

'I'm Gemma Howarth. I'm just watching the bar for Brad while he went to the hospital.'

'Is he all right?'

'Yes, he's fine. He took someone to hospital for me. I should really be back at home awaiting the surveyors to check the house.'

'I'm sorry. I shouldn't have been so rude. I'm Malcolm the chef.'

'That's OK, you weren't to know who I was when you found some stranger in the pub,' Gemma replied.

'Would you like something to eat? Homemade chilli and rice is today's special.'

'That sounds great, thank you.' Gemma smiled at him, taking her purse out of her pocket.

She checked the price of the special

and put the correct amount in the till.

Malcolm returned after a few minutes, a plate of chilli and rice in one hand and garlic bread in the other. It smelled delicious. Until then she hadn't realised how hungry she was.

'Thank you,' she said as she took the plates over to one of the tables.

The food didn't touch the sides, as Gemma's aunt would have said. Brad arrived as she was taking her empty plate into the kitchen.

'Don't you have bar staff?' she asked.

'Yes, but some days when it's quiet I don't. They will be in tonight and tomorrow on my day off, and I always have staff all day Sundays. Why do you ask?'

'I just wondered, that's all,' Gemma replied.

'Daisy is fine and said she would love a visit from you,' Brad said. 'They are keeping Mrs Longmire in and will test to see what she has taken, although the doctors think you're spot on and that she has ingested some poison.'

He took the empty plates from Gemma, placing them on the counter, then brought her into his arms and held her tight. He kissed the top of her head gently. He would have liked to kiss her properly but felt that might be being pushy. He hadn't known her long, but Brad knew she was the girl for him — all he had to do was tell her.

Brad held her at arm's length and looked at her. She was wearing a baggy purple jumper and jeans and her hair was tousled. She had rushed around so much today it was as though she had forgotten to take care of herself because she was too busy worrying about others.

'Brad, I need to talk to you.'

'Sounds serious, Gem.'

'Mr Bates was in here earlier and told me he was paid to put pressure on the owners of the cottages. He said he had been told my aunt's cottage was to be the first one sold off. But that would mean she would have to be out of the way for them to buy it.

'I don't think anyone read her diary in which she says she wanted to come and live with me. But his threatening letters hadn't scared anyone to sell, so the only way to get hold of those cottages would be to kill people.'

'That doesn't make sense.' Brad frowned. 'Mrs Miller didn't live in the cottages; she lived around the corner.'

'No, it doesn't, but it's not about that. I know what it's all about and I'm going to catch the killer, but I need your help. Do you have a spare mobile? I may need you in an emergency?'

'I think I do upstairs somewhere. I can try to find one for you,' he said with a smile which didn't reach his eyes.

'I'm going to go to the hospital to see Daisy and Elizabeth,' Gemma told him. 'I won't be more than a couple of hours. Will you come around later? I need to ask them a few questions and I will have it all figured out.'

'Gem, I've just found you and I don't want to lose you.'

'You won't.' She stood on tiptoe and

brushed her lips gently across his, then she moved back and left him standing in the middle of the bar.

* * *

Gemma was going to be a handful, Brad was sure, but he would love every minute of it.

While she was gone and it was quiet, he decided to do the books. He kept a book behind the bar and then transferred everything to his main account book upstairs.

Taking his mobile out of his pocket, he texted one of his bar staff — a girl called Annie — and asked if she would come in early to help with the bar. Tonight he had an Elvis impersonator on and he thought it would be busy.

The afternoon came and went, and Gemma never came back to the pub. While he had waited for her he had polished the brass cauldrons and dusted all the old books he kept on a shelf.

He was getting worried the longer Gemma stayed away. Once Annie got here he was going to go and see if Gemma was at home and then phone the hospital.

Annie arrived after an hour. Meantime, Brad had been pacing the floor.

'Annie, I need to go out,' Brad said sharply.

Taking a deep breath to calm his nerves, he left the pub and crossed the street to Gemma's cottage. He knocked on the door and waited, but there was no answer.

He thought Gemma might be around the back, trying to sort out the little garden, but she wasn't there, either.

He rooted around in his pockets for his mobile and rang the hospital to ask if anyone had been to see Daisy. When the nurse on the other end told him no, his fear increased.

Seeing Edith sitting on the bench by the village green, he made a beeline for her.

'Edith, you haven't seen Gemma, have you?

'Not since earlier I haven't.' She sounded apologetic.

21

Sadness in his Eyes

Brad checked Daisy's house. It was in darkness, and no-one had disturbed Stan's repair to the back door that Brad had broken.

Day had turned into dusk. He should be back at the pub, but he was really worried about Gemma. She had said she'd an idea but she had told him she would be back. Where was she?

What had she said? That it wasn't ever about the cottages? So what was it about? Brad didn't have a clue — he was no good at that sort of thing. Brad knew he was more of a hard man type guy. He wouldn't take aggro from anyone — except Gem maybe, he thought. He smiled. She was tough, yet on the inside she was as soft as melted chocolate.

Brad checked his watch. The Elvis impersonator was due at any moment and he needed to be there.

Maybe Gemma would come around later. Perhaps she had been held up. That's it, he decided, she had gone shopping in town after the hospital.

But she hadn't even reached the hospital. The nurse on duty had told him Daisy hadn't had a visitor since he had been that morning. Brad had broken the visiting hours' rule, but the nurses had been pretty accommodating.

Brad walked back around to the front of the house just in time to see Stan's truck show up.

Jogging over to the van, he banged on the door. Stan rolled down the window.

'What's the problem, lad?'

'Stan, do you have a key? Gemma's missing, and I need to check to see if she's hurt.'

Come on, Brad, he told himself, missing is going a bit far. She could be in town. Except by now all the shops would be closed and visiting hours were nearly over. No-one from the hospital had rung to say she had shown up.

'Lad, your lassie will be all right. I bet she has just caught up with a friend.'

'Stan, Gemma only has a few friends round here, one of whom is in hospital and the other one you're talking to.'

He caught the sadness in Stan's eyes and Brad wondered if Stan didn't have anyone either. He didn't wear a wedding ring and never talked to them about family. Brad hated to see anyone alone in the world.

The pub needed a lot of work doing to it and so did the cottage he was buying to live in. Perhaps Stan would like to live in the flat above the pub — it was much bigger than a single person would need.

'I'll let you in — only because it's you, mind.'

'Thank you, Stan.' Brad hung back while Stan unlocked the door.

Once the door was opened he ran upstairs, checking the two bedrooms and bathroom. Nothing!

'Gem, where are you?'

Stan called from downstairs saying she wasn't there, either, but her handbag was.

Brad jumped down the stairs two by two.

'Stan?' he shouted.

Stan came out of the living-room looking puzzled.

'Why are you so worried?' he asked.

'I don't know, I think it was just something she said earlier today,' Brad said, running his hand through his hair. 'I think she may be in trouble, but I could be totally wrong.'

'Look, lad, I'm sure that Gemma is fine, and she'll turn up soon.'

Brad could tell Stan was as worried as he was, yet the man was doing his best to reassure him.

'Stan, I want to ask . . . you seem to care about Gemma, too. Can you tell me why?'

Stan shifted around and looked extremely uncomfortable.

'I . . . I'd rather not.'

Brad looked closely at his eyes. They were the same shade as Gemma's. His hair was the same colour, too. Could they be related? But Gemma's folks died a long time ago when she was small, didn't they?

'OK, you don't need to tell me, but I think I have just figured it out. Why don't you come across to the pub and listen to the Elvis impersonator that we have on tonight?'

'Sure, it's better than going back to an empty flat. Not been the same since my sweetheart passed on.'

Brad felt sorry for him. Stan seemed like a genuinely nice bloke, and he really did seem to care about Gemma, too.

'Come on, I'll buy you a drink. I think you're right. Gem will show up.'

'That's the spirit, lad.' Stan slapped him on the back.

Brad and Stan left Gemma's cottage. Brad still didn't have a good feeling about the situation and he hated to feel so helpless.

Where are you, Gem, he thought to himself. He didn't have time to dwell on it once they reached the pub. It was coming up to seven o'clock and the pub was about to be a nightmare for the bar staff.

On the other hand, it would be great for his new house project. Brad had outgrown the flat over the pub — or was it his things that had?

22

Terror in the Darkness

Gemma lay on the cold hard floor of the crypt. Her head hurt and so did her ankle. She had never felt such excruciating pain.

Her hands had been tied and her eyes blindfolded. She couldn't even remember who had pushed her down the stairs. She must have banged her head and lost consciousness, and when she awoke she couldn't see anything except darkness.

She had been speaking to Edith, Gemma remembered that much, but about what? Daisy, yes, they had talked about that and Mrs Miller. Had there been anyone around whilst they spoke?

Edith had been sitting on the bench by the village green. Mrs Withenshaw was watering the bucket of cut flowers they had outside the shop. Thomas was coming from behind the church with his wicker basket, which she remembered was empty. The church door was open and Thomas had gone straight in, perhaps to see the vicar about Sunday.

There had been a few other villagers walking about at that time as it had been nearly pick-up time at the local school.

Gemma was cold even though she was wearing her thick jumper. She knew from a past visit down here that the walls were encased in stone. When she had looked in earlier a coffin lay in the middle of the room. That's when everything had gone black. Someone had pushed her down the stairs.

She must have hit her head on the way down and twisted her ankle. Finding she couldn't move her hands or see was so scary. No-one knew where she was.

Gemma tried crying out, but her voice just seemed to echo around the room. Would her voice be heard through the huge wooden door.

Why hadn't she told Brad where she was going? She would have kicked herself if it didn't hurt so much. The one thing that was going through her mind was that Stan, her new handy man, was possibly her father.

Gemma smiled. Despite her situation, it would be nice to have someone.

Gemma turned on her side and tried rubbing the blindfold off. It was slow going, but after what seemed like an age she managed to push it from her eyes.

Gemma tried to make some sense of her surroundings.

There were no windows and the only light coming into the room was from the cracks in and around the door. She had heard the lock turn, so unless someone came into the room she was here to stay.

Six small stone stairs had led down to the bottom of the unconventional crypt. Several spiders scurried along the floor.

A large wooden coffin lay in the

centre of the room, stacked high with old prayer books and papers. Against the brick wall at the far end of the crypt about 20 folded chairs were stacked.

Gemma could only see shadows with the help of the cracks in the door. It felt like more of a place to store excess things for the church than a place to keep a family vault.

Whoever had pushed her had been strong, but she hadn't seen the person's face.

Gemma tried to stand but her ankle gave way. The pain was excruciating and try as she might she couldn't stand up.

Pulling herself into a sitting position, she shuffled on her backside towards the wall nearest the door.

Brad had suggested that she should buy a mobile phone but Gemma being Gemma didn't listen to anything he had said.

What did Aunt Clara say? You can give someone advice, but it didn't mean they had to take it. This was one of those times she wished she hadn't been so stubborn, saying that a phone contract was a luxury that she couldn't afford.

She had asked Brad if he had a spare phone and he was going to hunt for one of his old ones for her but hadn't done so yet.

Mr Bates had given up on his bogus factory plan. What he had really wanted was some sort of treasure and to buy up the properties for some unknown person. They hadn't found anything in any of the cottages, but it didn't mean that the time capsule wasn't there — it was no doubt under someone's garden. Gemma would have to look a bit harder, that was all. So, if it wasn't him, then who?

Being stuck in here gave her time to think. Someone had killed her aunt and Mrs Miller, and had tried to poison Daisy and Mrs Longmire.

The bake off — that was what it was all about. How obvious it was now! Unless Gemma was completely off track, Mrs Withenshaw had the most to gain by having her rivals out of the way, but she wasn't strong enough to shove Gemma down the stairs and pull the heavy bar across the door.

But Gemma knew a man who was strong enough and who would be sneaky enough to concoct a plan just like this.

Now all she had to do was get out of this wretched room and get help. Surely if people knew she was missing then they would call the police.

A loud clunking sound was followed by a loud crash. Gemma shuffled towards the folding chairs and tried to sink into the wall. Her heart pounded in her chest.

Had whoever pushed her into the crypt come back to finish her off?

23

The Truth is Out

Gemma had no idea how much time had passed from this afternoon when she went into the church.

Just as she was giving up all hope of being rescued, the door creaked open and Gemma was blinded by the light flooding into the room.

'Gem, are you down here?'

'Brad! Down here — I've hurt my ankle,' she shouted back, her voice shaky.

Gemma could see his shape clearly in the light now pouring through the door, but from where she sat, half hidden by the stack of chairs, Brad's face wasn't visible.

His footsteps echoed on the concrete stairs. It seemed to take an age for him to reach her.

'Brad, be careful,' she shouted.
Brad ran towards her.
'Put your arms around me and I will get you back to your house.'
Gemma shivered.
'I think someone poisoned all those people and I think I've figured out why. The only thing I am not sure of is if they had help to pull it off,' she said.
Brad lifted her off the floor with ease and carried her gently. Gemma was reminded of Richard Gere carrying Deborah Winger in 'An Officer And A Gentleman', except this was no film; this was real life and her life was in danger.
'Gem, what on earth were you thinking?'
'What? Someone tried to hurt Daisy. I've already lost someone I cared about — did you expect me to lose another?'
'Yes, well, I don't want to lose someone I care for, either.'
Gemma found herself smiling despite everything that was going on. It was the

nicest thing anyone had said to her in a long time. Brad carried her out of the church down the stone path and across to her cottage.

Looking around her, Gemma realised that it was Sunday and she must have been down there for two nights. The fete was still going on around them, the green packed with people all standing around the various stalls. It looked like the Rose Queen and her attendants were having a great time. The Queen was dressed in a pink dress with a little tiara.

It took Brad ten minutes to get her back home and settled in the living-room, her foot elevated on a footstool.

'Do you have any bandages?' Brad asked as he hunted through the old sideboard.

'There may be some in the kitchen cupboards. I haven't cleared them out so if Auntie Clara had some they will be in there. Can you see if there are any painkillers, please?'

Brad put his hand on her shoulder

and gave it a little squeeze.

'Gem, stay there and I will see what I can find.'

It wasn't as though she could go anywhere — not without help. Gemma sat staring at her aunt's bake-off trophies that sat on the sideboard.

'Brad!' she shouted.

'Gem, what's wrong?'

'I've had an idea these murders and poisonings are all to do with the bake-off. Mr Bates was just a distraction. We need to tell the police and let them know what we think. Surely they will be able to investigate them?'

'I think you should phone Stan first to tell him you're OK. He's been worried sick about you for two days.'

Yes, Gemma thought, it would be the right thing to phone Stan. The person she was going to trap could wait — especially as word would have gone round by now that Brad had carried her out of the church.

'Will you please get me the phone.'

Brad disappeared into the hallway

and when he came back a few minutes later he had her address book and the phone.

'You make your call and I'll go and grab some bandages and make you a cup of tea and a sandwich.'

After he had left her alone, Gemma dialled Stan's number.

'Stan, it's Gemma. Would you be able to come over to my house? Yes, I'm home — a bit worse for wear but I'm OK. I think we need to talk.' Gemma put the phone down and looked at the picture of Aunt Clara she had put up on the wall. 'Thanks for telling me the secret,' she said quietly.

'I found some bandages,' Brad said as he came back into the room.

Kneeling down, he wrapped her foot up and then said he would call the police.

'No, not just yet — wait until Stan's here and then we can solve two problems. Besides, I need you both for my plan.'

'Gem, whatever you are thinking of

doing — don't,' Brad pleaded.

'Brad, I know I'm right. Trust me, please.'

Of course he trusted her, that wasn't in question, but whatever she was planning could go wrong. He had almost lost her over the past few days — what if he had never got her back?

Gemma looked paler than normal. He should really take her to the hospital, but knowing how stubborn she was he wasn't sure she would go until she had seen this through.

He made Gemma a quick sandwich and both of them a cup of tea. She ate without question or argument.

A loud knock on the door alerted them to the fact Stan had arrived.

Brad went and answered the door. Stan didn't have his key, as Brad now had the spare to Gemma's house. He had forgotten to give it back when they'd searched the house on Friday.

Gemma tried to sit up straighter in the armchair, but she was struggling and wouldn't ask for help. Stan stood in the living-room looking at Gemma.

'Hi, Gemma. Where have you been? We've been really worried about you.'

'I've been stuck in the crypt,' Gemma began to explain. 'Somebody pushed me down the stairs. I've been in there since Friday.

'I did something stupid and pretended to use the phone box,' she admitted. 'I said what I thought had happened. I knew someone was listening, so I thought I would trap them and say to the non-existent officer I was talking to that I would meet them in the crypt.'

Brad gave her a look. Hopefully she wouldn't do anything so stupid again.

'Gemma, I need to talk to you about something,' Stan said.

'You don't need to tell me anything. Not if you don't want to — besides, I know your secret.'

Stan looked horrified.

'What do you mean?'

'You're my dad, Stan. Aunt Clara said so in her diary. She also said that, although you had me first, you and Mum were meant to get married when she died.'

'I'll go if you want me to. I'm so sorry I wasn't around for you when you were little. I'd just lost the one person I loved and then it seemed too late to enter your life.'

Brad looked at Stan. The poor man was close to tears. Would Gemma tell him to go?

'Stan, I'd stand up and give you a hug, but I've been ordered to stay put.' Light filled Gemma's eyes as she opened her arms for Stan to go to her. Like lightning, Stan was by his daughter's side.

'So I suppose you will get someone else to finish the house?'

'Not at all! I've got my dad to do it.' Gemma kissed Stan's cheek and started to cry.

'Hush, little one. We have all the time in the world to make up for lost time.'

'Yes, Stan, we have.'

'You know, lassie, I'm not sure about

your choice of boyfriend. Brad's such a worry wart.'

Brad was horrified, but then Stan laughed and turned to him.

'She couldn't have picked anyone better.'

'Hey, I haven't picked anyone yet!'

Brad's heart sank — that wasn't what he had hoped Gemma would say.

'The problem, Stan, is that this one hasn't even asked me out yet,' Gemma added.

The way she looked at Brad melted his heart.

'Oh, I'm sure I can solve that problem. But don't we have a more pressing issue?'

Gemma had seemed to forget that for a moment. She nodded.

'Stan, Brad, will you both sit down? OK, I saw Thomas as I was using the phone, or at least while I was pretending to. I said that I would meet the police by the door to the crypt, and then I went over to the church and waited. The next thing I knew I woke up in the crypt with my hands tied and a blindfold around my eyes.'

Gemma took a deep breath then continued.

'At first I thought it was to do with the cottages and Mr Bates's idiotic plan to build a factory in the middle of the village. Or his quest for treasure, which I am sure he knew all along was a children's time capsule.'

'But why kill Mrs Miller?' Brad asked.

'That's what changed my mind about what the real reason was. What do my aunt, Mrs Miller, Elizabeth and Daisy have in common?'

Brad didn't answer. He had no idea what she was going with this. He didn't have to think as Gemma gave him the answer.

'They all participate in the bake-off. For that matter, who has won today?'

'I don't know. I've not bothered with the fete today and Annie did the beer competition for me.'

'Stan, could you go and see who got

the silver cup, please?'

'Sure, lassie, I will do. Back in a jiffy.'

Stan left Gemma and Brad alone.

'Gem, would you like to go out sometime?'

'Is that an offer, Brad?' She batted her eyelashes at him and he fell in love with her all over again. He wouldn't say that to her yet — perhaps after they'd had a few dates.

'Do you know who the murderer is?' he asked her suddenly.

'Yes, I think I do. I will have a better idea if Stan comes back and tells me who has won.'

The clock on the mantelpiece struck the half hour and Stan still wasn't back.

Just as Gemma and Brad were getting concerned, Stan came back into the cottage,

'Daisy won, is that a problem?'

'No. It's just a good job that Daisy is safely in the hospital and out of harm's way,' Gemma said.

'So are you going to put us out of our misery and tell us what this is all about?'

‘It’s all about trophies and someone who wants to be the best baker in the village. Do you know anyone like that, Brad?’

Brad looked confused. She saw how his brow knitted together but he didn’t answer.

‘It was Thomas who murdered Mrs Miller, and I am sure that he was the one who pushed me down into the crypt. As for Mrs Withenshaw, I’m not sure what part she or Margaret took, but I am sure with a bit of digging the police can find something.’

‘Gemma, you can’t go around accusing people of murder.’

‘Brad, you have to trust me. Just call the police and see what they say when they come. Tell them to come in an unmarked police car and park around the back. They need to come in through the back door. I’m right. We need to go across to the bakery with the police and catch them before they get rid of the evidence.’

It seemed crazy what Gemma was

saying, Brad thought. Did she have any idea what would happen if she accused the wrong person? Wasting police time; wrongfully accusing someone of murder.

PCs Anderson and Morgan came within the hour.

'I hope that this is important and you're not wasting our time again, Ms Howarth.'

'No, I think you need to check out Thomas's bakery and Margaret Withenshaw's shop.'

PC Morgan stood as straight as a statue.

'What makes you say that?'

'Look, PC Morgan, on Friday I was shoved into the church crypt and was left there for two days with no way out. I had been blindfolded and my hands tied. I managed to get the blindfold off but not the hand restraints. The door had been locked. I'm lucky I got out. The fact that I did is only thanks to Brad.'

'Why didn't you call the police to

report her missing?' The officer turned to Brad.

'I wasn't sure she was missing — she could have gone back to London for whatever reason. I got a telephone call to say that Gemma was in the crypt.'

'Man, or woman?'

'Woman. She had muffled her voice, so I couldn't really tell who it was,' Brad said.

'PC Anderson, I am sure that whoever pushed me was a man,' Gemma said.

'You think? That isn't much to go on.' PC Anderson turned away.

'I have a plan to catch the killer. I need you to have faith in me and stay here and out of sight until they come.'

'Gem, this is crazy, and it isn't going to work,' Brad insisted.

'Yes, it will,' she said with a smile. 'Brad, would you pass me the phone, please.'

Gemma took the proffered phone

and dialled the number she had memorised.

'I have had a bit of an accident and can't walk. Yes, a twisted ankle, I fell down some stairs in the church. Could you bring me some milk, a fresh bloomer and some washing powder?' Gemma found herself nodding. 'Yes, of course. Just let yourself in.'

PC Anderson paced the living-room.

'Whatever it is you're plotting could go wrong.'

'I know, but please trust me.'

The two police officers looked at each other and then nodded.

'Gem, this is dangerous.' Brad stared intently at her. 'You can't even walk.'

She placed her hand on his arm, and looked into his worried face.

'Brad, I know it's them. My auntie died when there was nothing wrong with her, Mrs Miller was found dead in the graveyard after being hit on the head, then Daisy and Mrs Longmire — both of them are still in the hospital.'

'Gem, you don't have to worry, the

doctors said they would be OK. They just need to stay in the hospital a bit longer.'

Gemma pulled a thread from the chair arm, nervously twirling it in her fingers. Putting herself in danger was something she hadn't really done before. The whole plan might work, but if it didn't she was worried about what could happen. She could be the next victim.

Brad propped the front door open before taking one of the police officers upstairs to hide, whilst Stan and the other officer hid in the kitchen.

Gemma's nerves jangled, and she felt sick to the stomach. This had to work. Gemma wondered if she had watched one too many episodes of 'Murder She Wrote'. Imagine thinking she could solve this crime where the police had failed.

Suddenly, there was a knock on the door and a male voice shouting.

'Hello!'

'Come in, Thomas,' Gemma shouted back.

Thomas walked in, still wearing his white apron and carrying a wicker basket filled with her order.

'I'm sorry I can't get up. Thank you for bringing this over for me,' Gemma said.

Thomas handed her the basket.

'It's no problem.'

Gemma looked at the basket and wondered what had been put in the bread — or did he have something else hidden in there? She eyed him carefully as he put the basket down on the sideboard.

'Why did you do it, Thomas?' she asked.

'Why did I do what?

'Kill my aunt and Mrs Miller.'

Thomas stepped towards her, his hands behind his back as though he was reaching for something. Panic filled her entire being. Would the police and Brad stop him from doing anything?

'What are you talking about?' Thomas demanded. 'Who do you think you are accusing?'

Shuffling in her seat, Gemma became

more uncomfortable the nearer he got to her.

'You pushed me down into the crypt. After the women's meeting you lured Mrs Miller to the back of the church and hit her over the head before covering up her body with tarpaulin. You tried to poison Daisy and Mrs Longmire — just like you did to my aunt.'

'I did nothing of the sort.' Thomas glared at her.

'I know it was you. You baked bread laced with poison. First you killed my aunt and then you tried killing Mrs Longmire the same way. As for Daisy, you picked death caps and gave them to her in her order.'

Gemma stared at him but Thomas hadn't flinched.

'You overheard me talking on the phone and knew that I was arranging a meeting in the church,' Gemma continued. 'You heard me because you had been watching what I do and where I go. Mr Bates told me all about the plan to buy the houses, and at first I thought it was all to do with the houses. Then I realised that what the victims all had in common was that they entered the bake off.'

'You're too nosy for your own good.'

Thomas whipped off his belt, folding it in half. A snapping sound resonated around the room.

'Why did you kill them?' Gemma flinched and held up her arm to protect herself.

'They were in the way, I had to kill them and now I will kill you.'

He really was going to kill her.

'The stupid bake off — that's why you killed them all? So your mother-in-law would reign supreme?'

'Have you any idea what she is like when other people win? It was all her idea in the first place, getting rid of the competition, hiring Mr Bates to threaten them all into selling the cottages so she could knock them all into one and own the biggest house in the village.'

Gemma gasped as footsteps bounded

down the stairs and PC Morgan, Anderson and Brad appeared in the living-room doorway.

Both officers grabbed Thomas at the same time.

'Thomas Atkins, you do not have to say anything, but it may harm your defence if you do not mention when questioned something that you later rely on in court. Anything you do say may be given in evidence.'

'Are you all right, Gem?' Brad asked gently as the police left with Thomas in handcuffs.

'Yes, I'm OK, just shocked. I didn't even think it would work.'

'How did you know it was him?'

'When the person shoved me, I caught a glimpse of something tied around their waist. It was unusual to see a bow at the front rather than at the back. I recognised it as Thomas's apron. I don't know anyone else who wears an apron like that.

'Then Aunt Clara's diary had snippets of conversation she'd heard and written down about the way Mrs Withenshaw was with everyone. Then Mr Bates wanted the cottages. When I called the estate agent's they hadn't heard of a Mr Bates.' Gemma paused and waited until she received nods of understanding from the three people in her living-room.

'They should have known the big developers, but it was like he didn't exist. I have a feeling that Mr Bates is not his real name, either. Then I made the connection that all the victims entered the bake off and that the cottage thing was a red herring.'

'What I still don't get is where Margaret comes into this,' Brad said.

'She doesn't. I doubt Margaret knew anything — or if she did she would have been too scared of the other two to say anything. Margaret will be safe now. I have a feeling that they would have found a way to rid themselves of her if she had talked to the police. Now she can without any problem.'

'Well, it's over now,' Brad stated

matter-of-factly.

'I best leave you two lovebirds alone for a bit,' Stan said. 'I'll be over at the pub when you're ready and, Brad, I'll let you buy me a pint.'

He left Gemma and Brad alone.

'Are we going to tell Daisy she won the bake off?' Brad sat on the sofa opposite Gemma. 'I can't believe that you cheated and got away with it.'

Gemma felt guilty about cheating, but it was better than Mrs Withenshaw winning.

'Yes, we'll go and see Daisy in the hospital and tell her the great news.'

'Listen, Gem, I've been wondering if you're ready to go on that date with me? After all the excitement you may need to relax a little bit.'

She thought it was cute how tongue-tied he was.

'I'd love that.' She grinned. 'Maybe you'll let me thrash you at bowling when my ankle is better.'

'Oh, yes, I'm sure you will. I think we need to take you to A and E to have your foot X-rayed.'

'It's only a sprain,' she insisted.

'But you still need to get it checked out,' he insisted. 'Come on, let's get you into the car.'

Once she was in the car, Brad set off for the hospital for the umpteenth trip of the week.

It seemed impossible that she had managed to work out who murdered poor Mrs Miller and her aunt. Gemma was glad it was over and that the murderous crew had been arrested and would be charged.

The traffic lights were against them. As they stopped, Brad turned to her.

'Do you fancy going on a murder mystery weekend? I'm sure we can find some trouble for you to get into.'

'Sounds good to me.'

Other titles in the
Linford Romance Library:

HERE COMES THE BEST MAN

Angela Britnell

When troubled army veteran and musician Josh Robertson returns home to Nashville to be the best man at his younger brother Chad's wedding, he's sure that he's going to mess it all up somehow. But when it becomes clear that the wedding might not be going to plan, it's up to him and fellow guest Louise Giles to save the day. Can Josh be the best man his brother needs? And is there somebody else who is beginning to realise that Josh could be her 'best man' too?